The Island the World Forgot
Torture Magic Novel 3.4 (32)

By Douglas Todt

First Edition (2022)

The Island the World Forgot
Torture Magic Novel 3.4 (32)

By Douglas Todt

The Island the World Forgot
Torture Magic Novel 3.4 (32)
By Douglas Todt

Tie-in Books
Society of Jack-O'-Lanterns, books # 1-5

Chapter One
Escape!
May 25, 2020

"We've been forgotten, haven't we?" asked Ashley of the team.

"No. But being in prison feels that way — prison anywhere. And no matter what the Consortium says, this Martian Best Western that looks like a leftover set from the *Prisoner* is a prison," said Geneva Kane with clear agitation.

"I'm with her," said Thunder.

Geneva Kane and her fellow paranormal prisoners on Mars were sitting in the lounge, which looked like a rec room basement in the bottom of a church, playing poker on Monday, May 25, which was Memorial Day on Earth. On Mars, it was just another day in captivity along with the rest of the people the Consortium felt threatened their plans on Earth. They had all been transported to Mars, where even if they left the facility, they had nowhere to go.

Theoretically.

But Geneva and a handful of her fellow captives — Ashley McMillian, her partner the Australian John Bogut a.k.a. Thunder, Crystal Jordan, and Judges 1040A and 1040EZ — had been trying to use Geneva's affinity for the probability cloud to trigger an escape by mixing her blood, influenced by PC tachyon particles, with geometric channeling. Geometric channeling used shapes to exponentially increase paranormal channeling power. Geneva's old friend Tripper

O'Sullivan was the expert on geometric channeling, but Geneva had learned a lot from him in the fifteen years she'd worked for Ops, so knew enough to handle this type of spell.

However, the attempts were risky. She had to drain her blood, and each attempt put her near death. In her first attempt, she felt she had reached her sister Medina. But it took her three weeks to recover from that attempt.

The attempts were getting easier, but she still needed two to three weeks to recover. The waiting was getting on Geneva's nerves. The same was true of Thunder and Judge 1040A, a true, uh, A-type personality.

Geneva was clearly the leader of the team. Besides the fact that she was the granddaughter of Gerald Kane, one of the team that had killed Hitler at the end of World War II, she was by far the most powerful and had the natural charisma needed to lead. Now almost thirty-four, Geneva had matured considerably from the snotty teenager that had joined Ops more than a decade earlier. She was a mature, attractive, classy woman, although not exceptionally beautiful. She had wavy black hair that was straight on top with bangs in front. Her hair draped halfway down her shoulder. Her eyes were bright blue and her face slightly square shaped but attractive. Her smile was cute and occasionally sassy. Her body was not as shapely as some, but she was attractive, with lots of curves, especially her bottom, legs and hips. She was a proper weight for her five-and-one-half-foot frame, but not in great shape — she despised working out but was good with her diet.

Like the rest of the team, she had at some point crossed the Consortium, a group of businessmen, governments, scientists, and channelers that said they wanted to save the world from global warming but appeared to have plenty of other agendas at play, none of them good. Geneva had been sent to Mars prison personally by the leader of the Consortium, Calico Kelkirk, and some type of alien she controlled, a big glowing ball called Quotient.

Geneva always had hope. In 2016, she and Tripper had been blasted into a 'blank' dimension by the alien Blue Square and thereafter spent a year and a half in Hell. They made it back.

She wasn't easy to kill.

But the rest of the team . . . well . . . they didn't have her background or stamina, although at least Thunder, Crystal, and Ashley had been part of Special Operations, which was the government division that dealt with the paranormal. Ops normally had about two dozen paranormal agents in operation at any time, so having four of them stuck on Mars obviously cut down their pool of talent.

Ashley and Crystal were the typical type of paranormal, elemental channelers. They could use telekinesis to manipulate the ancient Greek elements of earth, air, wind, and fire. Thunder was a variant who could also channel a basic force, that being electricity. Geneva was in a realm far above them, because she was imbued with the ability to manipulate tachyons and affect probability, though unconsciously. She was also simply an advanced channeler and could use TK on objects other than the four elements, though manipulating those four was far easier.

Ashley was getting depressed. Geneva could tell . . . she was largely ignoring the conversations around her and spending more time in her room. Twenty-six-year-old Ashley had a wonderful, cute little bob cut. Her face was attractive and round, with light blue eyes, brownish and blonde hair in a fetching bob cut, and a body that was purely round. She had large breasts pushing even her bulky pink sweatshirt, and her jeans were tight on her shapely bottom. Geneva was a little jealous. Ashley had one of those bodies that made men drool, something Geneva had never been able to do.

Also twenty-six, Crystal was also starting to think this plan to portal Geneva home was a false hope. She was average height with a thin frame. Her hair was light brown and curled in a wavy fashion. Her eyes were light blue, and her face appeared doe-like and sweet. Her teeth were perfect, and she usually wore full make-up with pink blush and mascara.

Geneva worried about Crystal, who had been brutally tortured and enslaved by Zenith a few years ago, much as Meredith Patience had been. Crystal seemed stable now, but Geneva didn't know if her fortitude would hold up if things got very stressful.

Fifty-three-year-old Thunder was doing well. An Ops veteran who operated out of Australia, he'd been in tough spots before. He had a chiseled, weathered face with gray hair, blue eyes, and a pointed gray beard. He was a sturdy man, probably six-two and in the 220 range. When they had first shaken hands, she realized he was strong. Geneva wasn't worried about him, but it was clear he was also growing frustrated. For a man of action, hanging around what amounted to a Best Western in the middle of nowhere wasn't the best way to spend the day.

The two judges were opposites. One was a retired judge from St. Louis named Eddie Eske, also known as Judge 1040A. Next to him stood his brother, Marty, also known as Judge 1040EZ. The brothers looked very similar, almost twins but not quite. Both were tall and thin with long, thin mustaches. They were wearing sunglasses despite being indoors. As one might guess from the names, Eddie was a hard-nosed, Republican type, while EZ was laid-back and willing to smoke pot while he pondered a solution.

Judge 1040A was always cranky and always over the top, but he seemed to be pouting a lot lately. And like Ashley, he was spending more time alone in his cabin.

Only Judge 1040EZ seemed to be handling it well, probably because he'd been zapped to Mars with a big stash of pot in his suitcase, and since arriving he'd managed to cultivate it.

Ashley got up, got some coffee, returned and said, "I just feel like we're not getting anywhere . . . that something is going to happen to you."

"We *can't* give up. I'm close," said Geneva, leaning in. "On this afternoon's attempt, I want to try something different. But it has serious risk."

"At this point, I'm for it. I ain't been as miserable as a bandicoot like this since I was held captive by the Rattler in Sydney back in '08," said Thunder, taking out a cigarette but not lighting it in deference to Geneva's preferences. Instead, he chewed on the end.

Geneva studied him and cocked her head. "You know, I'm starting to think half of your stories are made up and the other half are from some comic book."

Thunder looked at her, then chuckled. "Sheila, you come back to Australia with me when this is over and you'll see what *real* Ops work is, right quick."

"I've said before, don't call me Sheila. Or broad. Or tart."

"Sorry," he said, but with a wink.

Ignoring their byplay, Ashley said. "That just eggs him on."

"Yeah, I know."

"He does read a lot," said Ashley with a smile. Then seriously she said, "What could be more of a serious risk than what we're doing now?"

Geneva looked at them. "I'm convinced I will not make it out of here without the *essential* need to escape. I somehow must trigger the *latent* probability cloud tachyonic changes in my blood to act. I have thought of a way to do it, but if it doesn't work . . . I will die."

"We kill you?" asked Bogut with a worried look.

She looked at Thunder. "Yes."

"No way," said Ashley.

The others were quiet. The judges looked at each other. Crystal looked like she might cry.

'I'm not getting any closer. I almost reached Medina on the first try. Then I almost reached Tripper. Then, twice, I almost reached my mom. But it's always *almost*, and almost isn't going to free us and save Earth." She paused. "I have to somehow get my subconscious to act. It's the only way."

Thunder put down his cigarette and said, "For what it's worth, I agree, Sheila . . . Geneva. How do you plan to do this?"

"Let's talk."

At what would have been noon on Memorial day, the team lined up in Thunder's room.

Geneva wore a white turtleneck, hip-hugging gray slacks, and turquoise booties. She looked grim.

They had drawn a perfect equilateral triangle on the floor. Thunder, Ashley, and Crystal would man the points. Geneva stood on a cinder block in the middle of the triangle, a noose above her, attached to one of the support beams in the room.

"Hope this isn't goodbye," said Thunder.

"It's not," said Geneva, but she didn't sound very confident.

Ashley, Crystal, and Thunder moved into position.

Geneva was inside the triangle, facing Thunder. The triangle had a floor area of twenty square feet, so Thunder would, as usual, use channeling to telekinetically fling a knife across the room and cut Geneva's leg to make her bleed. But this time, he would also use TK to use wind to prevent Geneva from trying to free herself from the noose once she jumped.

Crystal was crying. Ashley wasn't, but she had her eyes shut. Thunder merely grimly frowned. The Judges had said their good-byes and left, not wanting to be part of it in case it didn't work.

Finally, Thunder said, "You ready . . . Miss Kane."

"Yes. If this doesn't work, you three have to keep trying. Promise me."

"We do," said Ashley.

Crystal merely nodded, clearly too emotional to speak.

"On five, team," said Geneva. She refused to consider this the countdown to her death. She *would* survive. She was a Kane, and she had a world to save . . . to say nothing of kicking Calico's ass for sending her here in the first place.

Geneva stood on a cinder block. Around her neck, the noose felt like a constricting snake.

"Five . . . four . . . three . . . two . . . one."

Using TK and a knife, Thunder cut her leg to trigger the blood flow. At the same time, Geneva jumped off the cinder block and kicked it away.

The pain was intense and immediate as her air was cut off and blood was trapped in her head. She made a horrible face as she was slowly strangled . . .

The world started to go red . . . then black.

She tried to scream that the plan wasn't working, but nothing came out.

She couldn't breathe . . .

And suddenly, she was gone.

But she *wasn't* dead.

Chapter Two
Arrival

Geneva awakened to find herself staring up a tile ceiling with tiny holes, the type seen in department stores throughout the United States. Grimacing, she felt a little dizzy and rolled onto her right side. The noose was gone, and her bleeding had stopped.

Studying herself, she saw the knife had cut her pants, but the wound was healed. The noose around her neck had vanished, and her neck didn't even hurt.

Weird.

Now she could see she was lying on a polished, gray tile floor next to a large white planter that had a palm tree inside it. There were couches nearby, and she was in the middle of the corridor.

"Great. I portaled to Macy's," she muttered to herself.

Slowly, she got to her feet, still groggy. Once she was up, she saw the corridor was a cul-de-sac. Ahead was a large, folding door like the type pulled over department stores connected to end malls when closed. She turned in a full 360 and saw the corridor kept going as far as she could see, then turned to the right. It was very much like a shopping mall corridor except there were no stores in the corridor, just walls of various structure and color. The colors were all dark: gray, blue, black, and maroon.

"Not what I pictured," she said to herself, to hear herself speak. The silence was unnerving. She looked around for cameras but saw nothing.

There was nothing to do but advance. She was beginning to suspect she had portaled only across the settlement and was in some type of shopping or maintenance area on the Martian settlement in which she was prisoner. She correctly assumed the PC tachyons and the scenario had allowed her to instinctively heal herself.

Feeling stronger with every step, she moved down the corridor. As she neared the junction, she started to hear faint noise, like a crowd far away. There was no point in being cautious. She had to find out where she was, for better or worse.

As she rounded the forty-five-degree angle of the corner, she found herself in what had to be a middle-class mall, though not all the stores were open. Now she could hear a weird, altered version of a song that sounded vaguely familiar. It was, although she couldn't place it given her confusion, a remixed version of *Connected* by Stereo MCs.

But there were no people around. The first store on the right had a large red sign across the top and shoes on display. The wording on the sign looked to her like Russian. But she was fluent in Russian and had spent years working there looking for Golden Bear, so she knew instantly it was not actually Russian.

Her eyes widened and she felt her heart pound. Maybe she *had* made it back to Earth! Maybe this was some type of Eastern European country?

Racing into the store, she found a clerk wearing a red, buttoned-down shirt, white slacks, and a nametag marking him as Jay. He had glasses, pimples, and short blonde hair. He looked like almost any store clerk in any shoe store anywhere.

"Can you tell me where I am?" asked Geneva breathlessly.

He looked at her dumbfounded. She repeated the question in Russian, French, and Spanish.

Finally, the boy said, "I can tell quarto about nil."

Furrowing her brow, Geneva figured he was speaking English, but what did the other words mean? So she asked, "Name?"

"Tag Jackson."

Rolling her eyes, Geneva realized she wasn't getting anywhere. But she was in some type of mall, some type of place with a lot of people, so she had a simple solution.

She passed out.

Or at least, she faked passing out, dropping to the floor in a somewhat melodramatic fashion. Acting wasn't her specialty. Once on the floor, she laid limp.

"Goat Tardy!" exclaimed the boy, and she heard him call for help. "Medic one, Cardy shoes."

Within seconds, a security guard arrived. Geneva slowly pretended to awaken and studied him. He was a big, bald white man with a mustache and a beer gut who looked like he should've been running a comic book store instead of working security. His uniform was blue, and he had a badge.

"Miss? Can you hear me?"

"Uhhhhhhhhhhh, yes. I'm Geneva Kane."

"Can you sit up?"

With his help, Geneva mimed slowly sitting up. She looked at him and asked, "Where am I?"

"Uh, the mall."

Snapping irritably, Geneva asked, "The city, I mean."

"New Reykjavik." He looked puzzled.

"Where is that?" she asked.

"Lat 12 Long 636.6, on Mars. Colony Two."

Geneva was confused. "I'm still in the *prison* colony?"

The guard looked at the clerk and then back at Geneva. "You need medic concussion eval. Sit."

She sat. Shortly, two men in white coats arrived carrying a stretcher. Geneva stood and told them, "I can walk."

"Not recommended," said the taller medic.

Not wanting to argue, she simply rode in the stretcher and the golf-cart sized and shaped ambulance through the mall to a sub-corridor where there was a doctor's office. Inside was a short, elderly woman with a turkey neck wearing a white coat, clearly the on-staff doctor.

"Hello, I'm Doctor Kozlowski. Your identity card please?"

"I don't have one," said Geneva.

"Oh. Oh, I see," said the older woman, clearly puzzled. "Well, could you hop up on the table?"

The table was like any other in any medical office in the universe: cold, white cloth over the bench, and charts about virus and cold care. Geneva used the step and sat on the end of the bench, arms folded across her chest. "I fainted. I'm fine now. Where am I?"

"You don't know where you are?" asked the doctor worriedly, getting out a pen to check her eyes.

"Of course not or I wouldn't be asking. I'm lost. I've never been here before," said Geneva. "At least you speak English."

"Most of us here do," said the doctor. "Your eyes seem fine. No wounds. How did you cut your pants?"

"Oh, uh, not sure. My eyes are most fine and most pretty. But I still want to know where I am."

The doctor stepped back and leaned against the cheap counter. "You're in station one in Red Rome, of course."

"*Red Rome*?" asked Geneva, and then she threw out her hands in a gesture of annoyance and frustration.

"Red Rome in settlement fourteen. Mars."

Geneva's eyes widened for a second, then she slammed a fist on the bench. "Damn. I haven't gone *anywhere*!"

"Gone anywhere? From where?"

"From my stupid triangle," she said, clearly pouting now. "I don't get it. I should have shifted further."

The doctor looked worriedly at her patient. "I think we should try and get you to a bigger facility. You seem very confused."

"I am not confused. I'm just *highly* annoyed," said Geneva. "I'm trying to save the world from horrible things."

"I see. And you are?" asked the doctor, clearly thinking Geneva was hallucinating.

"I am Geneva Kane of Maine, Special Operations agent."

"Maine? Earth?"

"That is where Maine was the last time I looked," said Geneva dryly.

"We should get you back then," said the doctor with a frown.

Geneva's face lit up with more excitement than a child on Christmas morning. "How? You can do that? *Why didn't anyone tell me?*"

"It's just a matter of a shuttle, but I have to check the schedule."

Now Geneva looked perplexed. "Schedule? Shuttle? I thought this was a prison. That's what everyone has said."

"Prison? Miss, tell you what, please lie back and relax a minute."

Geneva was going to argue, but clearly they were both concerned about the information being exchanged. So she lay back and tried to relax by taking deep breaths.

It didn't work.

"Now, Miss Kane, I'm going to run you through concussion protocol. Obviously, you know your name, but I can't verify it anyhow. You have no ID. Do you know who the President of Mars is?"

"I didn't know Mars had one."

"The President of the United States?"

"Donald Trump . . . for the moment," she added, making a face.

"Trump?"

She looked at him and her eyes widened as it suddenly struck her. "You don't know Donald Trump?"

"Don't be silly. Everyone knows him. He's super rich. He's the guy who owns the New York Jets."

Suddenly, she threw her hands over her face and lay back on the table and cried out, "Oh, poooooooooooooooooooop!"

"Miss Kane, are you okay?"

Geneva suddenly jumped off the table. The shock was over. She had always been adept at transitioning from situation to situation, and she had to do so again. "I'm in a *parallel* dimension. This is Mars, right?"

"Yes."

"Makes sense," she said, biting at a callous on her left thumbnail. "I moved across *dimensional* space, not real space." Sighing, she said,

"Okay, that's still progress. Very well. Get me to Earth. I'm with Special Operations."

"What?"

"Never mind. Just start making calls."

Chapter Three
Reunion
5/26/20 Tuesday

"My goodness, I never thought I'd see *you* again!" said Geneva the next morning as she stepped off the shuttle at the spaceport on Miramar Air Force Base in San Diego and greeted Jennifer Saunders.

"Me either!" said Jen excitedly. Jen was normally controlled with her emotions, but tears leaked down her face as she raced forward to great her old friend.

They hugged. Geneva sniffled. "I'm so glad to see you!"

"Me, too!" said Jen, and she had tears. "I wish we could've talked more, but speaking on the shuttle channels isn't secure, and you dropped a code that is utmost security."

Geneva nodded, then she stepped back. "It's okay. Gosh, boy, well, you look good!"

Jen made a face. "I'm fat, stop lying!"

And she was. Jen had always been a little overweight in just the right areas, a very round girl, very attractive thought she didn't know it. Her long, brown hair was always messy. But she never looked fat. Now she looked like a cuddly play doll, at least seventy pounds overweight.

Geneva quickly said, "No, seriously, have you been working out? You look good, really!"

"Are you kidding? My weight training is *I wait for training*," said Jen, repeating a joke Anissa had told her.

Geneva laughed. "I love the outfit."

Jen wore a billowing yellow blouse to hide her weight gain, mixed with a royal blue undershirt, new jeans, and brown flats. She smiled. "Thanks. I love the space traveler look."

Geneva laughed. She was still wearing an orange jumpsuit, required for all space travelers. "The best thing you can ever do for me is get me out of *this* ridiculous thing!" Then seriously she said, "Then we must talk. The situation on our homeworld is grave."

"Sure. Ops now runs out of San Diego, so we have auxiliary facilities here at Miramar. Joshua Clegg and Colin are in a conference room down here," said Jen, leading Geneva down a corridor that had clean white tile, yellow security tape, and ended in a large metal door marked with warning signs. "It's military, secure."

"Good." Suddenly, Geneva was serious and grabbed Jen's shoulder. "Have you seen a big ball of light here called Quotient?"

"No." Jen was about to tell her about Radar's warnings, but Oscar internally indicated she should hold that information for the moment. As usual, Jen deferred to her mentor's feelings.

"Good." Geneva suddenly grabbed Jen by the shoulders "I've been in prison on Mars for months. Coming here was a miracle. Our planet, our entire race, faces terrible, terrible danger."

"Let's talk with the others," said Jen, and she started to open the door to the sterile conference room.

But internally, Oscar said, "You should tell her about Meredith now."

"Oh. Oh, I guess," said Jen, knowing what Oscar meant. Then she turned to Geneva and said externally, "Before we go in, I have some, well, shocking but good news."

"Believe me, on a day like this, you're got to have a *real* wildcard to pull that trick off," said Geneva dryly.

Jen hesitated, and then took a deep breath. "Meredith Patience . . . is . . . here and alive."

Geneva's jaw fell. "She is?"

"Yes."

"Is she hurt?"

"She was in a coma, but she's recovering well."

Geneva shook her head. "Well . . . *that* was some wildcard. My god. I . . . I *can't* believe it." She paused. "Wow." Then she hugged Jen and started crying.

"It's true," said Jen when they broke the embrace. "I mean, her life is weirder than mine, I guess. She's alive."

Geneva looked at Jen and smiled. "Jennifer, there is no one that has led a stranger life than you!"

Once upon a time, there was a woman named Jennifer Saunders who lived a quiet, sheltered life as a scientist. But Jennifer was *not* a fairy tale princess. Her entire life was defined by loss.

Jennifer was a pretty woman, though oblivious to this fact. In 1999, she joined Special Operations, the government organization that studied the paranormal. Jen was only twenty-two years old and fresh out of Stanford. At that time, she had unruly brunette hair that ran in waves past her shoulders, pretty blue eyes, and nice but chunky figure. Generally, she dress was . . . dowdy. But to Jen, her appearance was unimportant. Her life was her work.

Jennifer had never been gregarious. Her mother had died in a car accident when she was only five, and her father had just died a couple of months before she joined Ops, so she was alone. Once at Ops, she stepped in to carry on his work cloning a human with a soul. They were also studying Subject Six, the alien creature in a coma ever since the crash landing in '87.

The complex where Jennifer worked was buried underground in the remote Arizona desert. Jennifer liked this environment. She was focused on her work. Jen *enjoyed* the work. She loved science. It had rules and limits, no *emotion*.

Emotions terrified Jennifer Saunders. When only seven years old, she had witnessed her best friend, June, get murdered and dismembered by June's mother. The result was that Jen had developed dissociative identity disorder, creating seven alters that functioned on a subconscious level to protect Jennifer from the trauma. When joining Ops, she only knew of one alter: Patty, her little girl self.

Jen had also been molested by her uncle. He later attacked Jen and her roommate, Karen, in their dorm in Stanford. Karen later killed herself, traumatized by the attack. Uncle Bill had terminal cancer and died shortly after as well.

Suffice it to say, Jennifer did not trust people.

She trusted science.

In Arizona, she was successful in her enterprise. Robby was born, a clone with a soul, verified by an out of body experience during a medical emergency.

On April 16, 2004, Subject Six, nicknamed Insectia by one of the staff, woke up. She wasn't happy about having her DNA tampered with, having her soul damaged. She killed the forty-plus members of the compound, including Robby, and including Jennifer and her best friends and co-workers, Shauna Thompson and Allan Elliott. But Jennifer's D.I.D. protected her. Insectia was a bee-like creature, although technically more related to the order of hymenoptera, the wasp. Mentally, she was part of a collective consciousness with advanced telekinetic and telepathic abilities. Her telepathic attacks were blunted by Jen's unique D.I.D. framework. Jen survived.

So did Allan. He clandestinely had been working for the Consortium, a band of paranormals, businessmen and politicians that supposedly were out to protect the world from global warming. However, Allan had secretly bonded with Insectia, betraying the team.

Later, they found out Zenith, Oscar Clegg's torture magician ex-wife, had actually awakened Insectia in an attempt to ensure Jen would die and not threaten her plans. Torture magicians were the most dangerous of paranormals, ones that used the pain and adrenaline generated through torture to power telekinesis and other skills.

Two others survived the attack in the complex, although 'survive' was a relative term. Oscar Clegg, Jen's 78-year-old mentor who had a bald head and scruffy gray beard; and Anissa Radovich, a young nurse with chipmunk cheeks, curly blonde hair, and a buxom frame. Each had their souls somehow grafted to Jennifer's psyche. Their bodies were dead. Their souls were not.

Jen was now a 'soul' survivor, a very rare paranormal event. With Jen, Oscar and Anissa formed a team that stopped Insectia from breeding a new colony in the hills outside San Diego.

During the final battle, Insectia inadvertently infused Jen's friends Brent and Sheila with telekinetic powers. Jen also had a shard of Insectia's psyche fused to her mind, as Oscar and Anissa had been. Insectia was really named Jaye, the closest translation in our language, something Jen learned later.

About a year after the attack, Jen was working for General Emerald Jon Jameson and Special Operations. Jameson and Clegg had been friends for more than thirty years. Jen's mission was to protect a research project in Oklahoma. Unknown to anyone, it had already been secretly taken over by Zenith.

Using a gem that transferred the user between dimensions, although not space, Zenith displaced Jen into the nearest parallel world, a world where Zenith's plans succeeded. There, the parallel Shauna was murdered, and Jen went into a catatonic coma.

For a year, Anissa took over Jen's body and fought with the resistance in the parallel world. But they were losing. Badly. During this time, Clegg, trapped in Jen's psyche, completed a complex integration of Jen and her seven personalities: Patty was really a young, child version of Jen. They integrated with the system that included: Liza, a spiky-haired, nose-ring wearing teen who kept order; Prisoner, a girl locked in an asylum with no mouth so she wouldn't give away the secret of Uncle Bill's violations, a secret Jen had subconsciously repressed; Cara, a blonde young girl who held Jen's anger; Don, the sullen teen with messy hair who played basketball by himself; Honey, a very young girl; and Rudolph, a very young boy. They also integrated the aspect of Jaye's personality.

They returned to our world to escape a devastating combat loss in the parallel world in 2006 but had to return immediately.

Fully whole for the first time in her life, Jen spent the next four years fighting losing battles in the parallel world. Movement across worlds grew more complex as they grew more divergent. Jen changed, maturing form a scared young woman to a bold fighter.

Seeing defeat as inevitable in the parallel world, seeing millions killed and enslaved, Jen needed another plan. Jaye suggested calling her people, and in 2010 Jen returned to her and our world to call them, planning to then portal them into the parallel world — the ultimate surprise attack. But wary of Jennifer, Tripper O'Sullivan foiled that plan.

Jen returned to the parallel dimension a failure.

In 2014, Jen returned knowing from the parallel world and other sources that Zenith on our world was close to instigating another successful drilling project, one that would give her access to Soloman's Liquid and allow her plans of conquest to continue. Zenith was obsessed with security, traumatized by being held as a child in the concentration camps of the Nazis during World War II.

Soloman's Liquid imbued female TMs with immortality and changed males into crazed werewolf-like creatures, an unstoppable if short-lived army. It had obvious benefits for Zenith.

Jen helped Ops halt that project. Zenith was arrested and incarcerated in Atlantia, a hidden kingdom under the arctic ice, by its exceptional queen, Marrina.

Jen then realized she had a way to stop the parallel Zenith.

Which she did. With the aid of the parallel Joshua Clegg, Oscar's son, she saved the parallel dimension and together they rewrote it. But this action made it much less parallel to her native and our present Earth and made moving back and forth more or less impossible.

Or so everyone believed, until Meredith Patience arrived.[1]

---

[1] See TM 3.3 "Lack of Patience"

"Meredith alive . . . wow. Sam will be shocked." Then Geneva looked alarmed. "She was in combat right before she came here. Is she, well, all there?"

Jen quickly nodded. "She's healthy, but she was in a coma until just a couple of months ago. We've, ah, been trying to find a way to get me and a team back, because of what we found out from her, we figured Earth, our Earth, was in danger." Again, she held back Radar's warnings. That was too much to get into at the moment.

Geneva quickly overcame her shock. "It is, but not from *those* threats."

"She mentioned this man named Everett."

Geneva nodded. "Yes. He was an avatar, a probability cloud manifestation of the subconscious of that slime, David Mize."

"I remember him," said Jen irritably.

"Yeah. We stopped them, but the new threat we face . . . it's horrible."

For a moment, Geneva considered breaking the news about Sheila, Jen's oldest friend, but now she refrained.[2] It was news for everyone, but she also thought Jen would do better hearing the news with friends around for support. "Let's go inside, please."

"Sure."

They entered to a small conference room decorated with white cabinets, white tile, light blue walls, and a large picture window showing the runway of the spaceport, which at the moment was empty. Behind that was the brush of the Miramar property and some coastal clouds, much the same in the parallel dimension as it was in Geneva and Jen's native dimension.

At the table sat Joshua Clegg and Colin Ridgeway.

Now fifty-three, the Colin Ridgeway of the parallel dimension looked younger, showing few of the wrinkles and sagging typical of men his age. He had curly brown hair that looked like a wig but wasn't, sharp blue eyes, and a curt and almost manic manner. He was

---

[2] Sheila became one of the first victims of Quotient in TM 3.1 "Escape"

overweight by about forty pounds but hid it well. Today, he was wearing a yellow, collared shirt and black pants.

Now seventy-four, the parallel Joshua Clegg, son of Oscar Clegg, was a man with receding white hair, thick and black-rimmed glasses, wrinkling but handsome skin, and piercing blue eyes. He was in good shape. Wearing baggy brown slacks and a tight light blue shirt, he appeared to be some type of administrator. He had an odd accent, like someone who was born in England but had been in the States a long time.

"Well, well, well, Miss Geneva Kane. You don't call, you don't write, what is a man to think?" said Colin with a broad smile.

Geneva laughed. She had spent years in her Earth with her Colin, had been trained by him and travelled Europe with him. But she had also worked with the parallel Colin before the dimensions were essentially sealed apart from each other in 2016. She hugged him. "Your hair looks great."

"But of course."

Then she shook Joshua's hand. "Good to see you again, Mr. Clegg."

"Joshua, please. Have a seat. Cookies?"

Geneva grabbed the box of chocolate chip and started scarfing them down. "Thanks. I'm starving! It's been probably the most trying day since I got zapped to Hell."

"Hell?" asked Colin, arching an eyebrow.

Geneva looked at him and laughed. "I don't sit around knitting or looking at cat videos all day! But that is a story for another day. We have more urgent matters."

They sat and internally Oscar said to Jen, "I think she's hiding something . . . be ready."

"I don't think so, but I'll be ready," said Jen.

Geneva took a deep breath. Colin brought her a bottled water without her asking, knowing what she would want. She smiled and said, "Thank you, Colin."

"But of course. Now, how did you get here?"

She laughed. "O . . . M . . . G! Here is the story of my life in 2020!" Quickly, she said, "Back on January 5, I was sent to the Antarctic to recover, ah, the body of an Ops agent. I arrived with a team that included two of Golden Bear's agents, who turned out to be Calico and a man named Englehart." Fury crossed her face. "They turned on me, ambushed me, and kidnapped me for Kelkirk."

"Kelkirk! He's still around?" asked Jen, parroting words internally asked by Oscar.

"Not anymore — I'll get to that. Anyhow, in January, yes, he was. Uh, see, he was running the Consortium and diligently and, from what I have seen, quite sincerely trying to save the world from global warming. The problem is, what I found while his prisoner, is that he wants to do this by creating a colony on Mars."

"M'dear, you may not have noticed but that's *not* such a wild idea," said Colin with a chuckle.

"Oh, I've noticed, but your Mars and ours isn't the same. Anyhow, Kelkirk died while I was his prisoner."

"What?" interjected Jen.

"Yes. I don't know any details. Just that he died, and I found out Calico was his daughter. She and Englehart seemed to be in control. Calico wanted me to help them, but I refused, and after Kelkirk died, Calico then portaled me to a prison colony they had established on Mars." She ate a cookie and took a deep breath. "To make a *very* long and *very* trying ordeal very short, I and several allies finally used geometric channeling and the probability cloud aural traces in my body to portal here, although I was trying obviously to get back to *my* Earth."

"That . . . is amazing," said Joshua.

"How did they portal you to Mars?" asked Jen, a question she and Oscar both had.

"I don't entirely know. The found in the ice in Antarctica an alien that's this sort of big glob of glowing cookie dough named Quotient. But others were sent to Mars before Calico found Quotient. I don't know how she trapped them there."

"Well, using Mars as a prison is rather fanciful, I admit, although nothing like the stage play I was in back in '89, *The Keys of Maritime*," said Colin whimsically.

"Okay, go back," said Jen. "You talked of terrible danger. Living on Mars isn't dangerous. We've had colonies on Mars here since 2017. The Consortium has much less power here, and the advances in science Joshua and I inadvertently introduced with our rewrite of the blank slate dimension has moved us scientifically ahead. Likewise, we have no TMs like Kelkirk and Zenith inhibiting progress."

"That's not the case on our Earth," said Geneva, sipping water. "The problem isn't the solution of moving to Mars. The problem is *how* he intends to put it into practice. You see, like I was saying, the Kelkirks found a creature called Quotient to aid them. And Calico and her partners in the Consortium plan to use it to portal equipment, materials, and people to Mars."

"So he's found an enormous ferry," said Colin with a shrug.

Geneva quickly shook her head. "No, that's the problem. He isn't just a big bus. Quotient is a *monster*, some type of alien that's shaped like a yellow bowling ball and floats in the air. He powers all of this not only by killing people, but by killing them and absorbing their auras. *He destroys their souls*!"

Suddenly, she began to cry, which shocked them all. Geneva Kane was one of the most prestigious paranormals on either world. She had everyone's utmost respect and was one of the toughest people on the planet. But she came apart like a teenager.

Colin comforted her, but Geneva needed the emotional release. The months of torment being locked on Mars, the fear for her family and friends on Earth, the desperate attempts to escape and finally succeeding only to be on the wrong world . . . it finally overwhelmed her. For months, she had been the *one* person in the universe who knew of the danger to Earth and wanted to stop it. Now, having finally escaped, the pent-up emotions released in a flood.

Jen looked at Joshua. "Do we have a Quotient here?"

"There's a legend of such a being, killed by Marrina in 949. Never been seen since. I'd assume our rewrite took care of it if it still existed here, because part of the rewrite was stabilizing his Earth from arcane influence. But we'd have to research. Obviously, 949 was long before Zenith's influence, so the rewrite specific to eradicating her influence wouldn't apply. I wouldn't worry about it for now, though. The Consortium here is far different. There are no Kelkirks here, for starters."

"Good," said Jen. "Then let's deal with Geneva's problem first."

Colin rubbed Geneva's shoulders. She finally pulled her head up and wiped her eyes. "So . . . sorry. I just . . . it's been a difficult time."

"We understand," said Jen, putting a comforting hand on Geneva's. "I can't believe how brave you are, to hold up under all of this."

"I had no choice. I'm just . . . I'm so scared for my family, my friends, but all the innocents who will lose their souls. They're talking about snuffing *millions*. They're building the future on the blood of the innocent."

"We *will* stop them," said Jen with unusual forthright determination.

Internally, Oscar said, "Ask who the Ops agent was they found dead, please."

"Why?" asked Jen suspiciously.

"I think . . . it's important," said Oscar, correctly having guessed Geneva would conceal this only if it would personally affect Jen.

"Okay," said Jen internally, then externally she asked Geneva, "Geneva, I'm sorry, but who was the Ops agent killed in the first place?"

Geneva shot Colin a look. He had guessed as well, and he gave her a curt but gentle nod. Geneva then put her hand on Jen's and just gave her a look.

"Oh, no! *Oh, no!*" cried Jen.

And then she cried for a long time, consoled by her friends.

Chapter Four
The Plan

Two hours later, the team had moved to a downtown San Diego Ops office. Geneva had been given a change of clothes and now wore thick black pants, white boots, a light gray blouse that hung long and was cinched with a white belt, and a white jacket.

They were in a conference room that had a large, round table with a video screen insert and forty-six screens on the four walls, all viewing different news.

The team sat. Jen was still shaken by the news of Sheila's death, obviously, although at least she was consoled that Sheila took her own life to save her soul. Jen's face was stained with running lipstick and tears. Geneva looked weary but determined. Colin and Joshua looked concerned.

Geneva took the lead. "I think we're agreed we have to get back to our Earth, Jen."

"Yes, certainly. I've been trying ever since Meredith arrived, but now, I agree, we have to take any chance we can. You're the only one who knows the danger . . . other than Radar." Sheila's death made Jen realize she needed to put all the cards on the table. The stakes were far more serious than she had recognized.

"What's a Radar?" asked Geneva.

"Long story, but he's a seer — he's Meredith's uncle."

"Oh? I thought he was dead!"

"So did everyone, but he actually got zapped here by Zenith years ago. Anyhow, we can get into that later. He sees a danger of our worlds *merging* and said the big moment was coming in a few weeks, maybe a couple of months. That was in March. So it seems like your arrival is key. But for now, you keep going," said Jen.

Geneva gave her a look, then she said, "Very well. I had no luck using PC channeling to get back to Earth while stuck in that ridiculous Mars Best Western serving as a prison, but I got *here*. However, having Meredith here is a significant advantage. Jen, what is her situation? Did the coma damage her?"

"This should be a fun talk," said Anissa internally to Jen.

"Hush," said Jen internally. Then she looked at Colin.

The look between them told Geneva a great deal. "Okay, you two fought over *something*. What happened?"

Colin took a deep breath and ran his hand through his hair. Then he said, "We've had a rather . . . eventful 2020 ourselves. When Meredith arrived two years back, she was in her coma. Her mind was read by Ogg, the telepath, to find out what happened to her, how she wound up here. With the rewriting of the blank slate dimension by Jen and Joshua back in 2016, her arrival was an event that was seemingly impossible. While reading her, Ogg saw her kill . . . many people."

Geneva's face went rigid. She knew about Necra and many of the other killings and knew this was trouble. "I see."

"She was justifiably put on trial," said Jen. "Geneva, I can see it on your face. You know she committed crimes, deliberately hunted down and tortured to death people."

Geneva winced and put up a hand, then she looked at Colin. "How could she be on trial here? She's from a different planet."

"That's what *I* argued," said Colin, clearly irritated.

Shaking her head, she said, "Wait. *You* defended her? And you couldn't get the case dismissed because of that?

"I did argue it quite vehemently," said Colin, clearly embarrassed.

Geneva rolled her eyes. "No *wonder* you became an actor."

"Getting back to the point," snapped Jennifer, "she's a convicted killer and is prison. You knew of her murders, didn't you?"

"Yes. I . . . there were circumstances, Jennifer."

Jen glared. "Not to justify *that*." And suddenly she was angry, a rarity for Jen. "How could this have happened, Geneva? This is the sort of thing Oscar warned me about from the *very beginning*, that Ops worked under its own rules and did its own thing, that it could easily become the thing it fought. He never trusted Jameson because of that. Now I think he was completely correct."

Geneva was about to respond, clearly on the defensive, surprised by Jen's anger. But before she could proceed, Colin tried to stop a potential debate by interjecting the end of the story.

"Anyhow, we had a trial. I defended her and lost due to some chicanery by the prosecution, who turned out to be a robot," said Colin.

"A *robot*?" said Geneva with wide eyes.

"It's a very long story, but let's cut to the end. For now, until we can determine what having the prosecution being a robot does to the verdict, she's in prison," said Colin, clearly wishing to brush his failure as her attorney under the rug. "But, she wants to be there. She was ambushed in prison before, and we know there's a conspiracy at very high levels. We don't know everyone involved. She was willing to stay until the legal point is settled, hoping to get more information."

Geneva nodded and thought very quickly and very carefully. At least Colin's quick synopsis and the fact that Colin and Jen were together in this room told Geneva two important things about where her two allies stood; first, clearly they had come to a compromise. Second, they both were afraid of how Geneva might react.

And Geneva wasn't sure about how she felt. Geneva herself did not believe Meredith a murderer. She was fighting TMs, had killed only TMs, though Geneva obviously didn't know all the details. But she certainly didn't want to get into an ethical debate with Jen, because Geneva believed she needed Meredith and hence Jen to get back home. And . . . underneath it all, Geneva considered Meredith a friend. Perhaps a *troubled* friend, but clearly a friend.

It was a *very* delicate situation.

Geneva looked and spoke to Jen with just an occasional glance at Colin and slowly began to speak, her arms folded over the table as if she were a pastor trying to calm a grieving parishioner. In gentle tones, Geneva said, "Meredith was always an unusual case, Jennifer, because of her ability to portal. She was hunted by TMs like an animal. But beyond that, Zenith — and I would think you of all people understand the power Zenith had and her ability to cause destruction — completely warped her life when she was little more than a child. She was sixteen, Jen, when Zenith killed her parents, enslaved her sister as a zombie soul-slave, and left her in torment." Pausing, Geneva wiped away real tears. "I was roughly her age when I discovered my powers, saving my bloodhound from drowning. I had a wonderful family. I love my mother deeply, but I also had my grandfather to teach and guide me through my early days. I joined Ops and had Colin and Tripper and many other friends." She shook her head. "Meredith had *none* of that. She buried her grief, was forced to go on the quest to save her sister. In her quest, she was forced to do horrible, demeaning things to save her sister. And she *lost*. Her sister's soul was destroyed." She softly asked Colin, "Did those come out in trial?"

"Some."

She looked at Jen. "She sold her body. She sold her ethics. And in the end, all of her sacrifices *failed*. Beth wasn't rescued. Her soul was destroyed."

"I know that," said Jen, not sure what point Geneva was trying to make.

"I don't think you do, and that's my point. Meredith was never truly free. She was *perpetually* under attack from the minute Zenith ripped apart her family . . . I spoke with Sam about this not long after she killed Necra." Geneva cleared her throat. "Believe me, some in Ops wanted Meredith imprisoned as you had done. But . . . I did not believe that *justice*." She paused. "I don't condone killing. I believe in redemption. But at times, there is a point of no return." She added, "I may not have done the same things as Meredith, but I don't think she was guilty of a crime when she did them. Meredith faced battles we simply didn't."

Jen shot Colin a quick glance, but he was focused completely on Geneva as he said, "In what way? Just wondering if my failed defense missed some points."

"I never condoned Meredith's actions. But I have a sister, Medina, who I love very much even though she is very different from me and can be very annoying," said Geneva, rolling her eyes. "Now, I would like to think if I came home and found my parents dead and Medina enslaved to a torture magician, I would find a way to stop her and save Medina without taking lives. However . . . I don't really know that I could. I just *don't*. Meredith was constantly at war. My grandfather killed many paranormals, many normal humans during World War Two. Necra and Zenith . . . women like that, torture magicians like that, are never helpless, not even when aura blocked and bound. How many times have *we* escaped similar captivity? Like when I escaped Mize?"

"A few," admitted Jen reluctantly.

"Sam understood this. He also understood he was the only thing standing between her and the abyss, either insanity or even worse, her lashing out and turning on everyone and becoming a monster. The pain inside her was incredible — well, I guess she's alive, so it *is* incredible. Jen, I was sent to a blank slate dimension that had been consumed by Hell. Much of my memory of that place is lost . . . but I know what it's like to be at war in a world with no values. *That's* where Meredith lived."

Geneva fell silent, shaking her head.

Jen pursed her lips. "I understand your points. But I don't think that makes killing Necra, to say nothing of some of the others, justified. We'll have to agree to disagree." Then she looked at Joshua and Colin. "This is the danger of having an Ops, of operating outside the law. Someone should have stopped Meredith. If she couldn't stop herself, someone should have stepped up and done it for her."

"You seem angry," said Geneva.

Jen suddenly exploded in a very un-Saunders like rant, turning beet red as she slammed a fist on the table. *"Of course, I'm angry*! What happened with Meredith is just what happened to me! I sat in that complex in Arizona and experimented with a living being! I cloned Robby from Jaye without knowing *anything* about the consequences! I was arrogant and reckless and I was encouraged! *I was rewarded*! Until the day *she woke up and fucking killed us all*!" she said, shrieking now.

"Jennifer," said Joshua, putting out a hand to comfort her.

She knocked it away. "*Nothing* would be like it is today if someone had stepped up and said it was a *bad idea*. Nothing. That's what should happen when you have a procedure and a process and oversight. Ops is not that. Ops is so used to dealing outside the norm that it can't see the dangers."

She was calming down now. Oscar internally said, "You've made your point."

Jen understood and said calmly. "But . . . what's done is done." Then she started hard at Geneva. "I'm not surprised Sam didn't stop her. He's the figurehead. But I at least would have thought someone, maybe *you*, would have stepped up."

"In fairness, I was in Hell for a year and a half and a bit outside the day-to-day of Ops," said Geneva, not sure what else to say. Clearly, this was an issue Jen had to resolve on her own.

"Are you . . . okay? Still angry?" asked Joshua.

"No." And Jen stood and shook her head. "Just very, very *disappointed*." Then she took a deep breath. "But that's all in the past. It changes nothing."

Colin raised a finger. "One point here. One thing *has* changed dramatically." He pointed at Geneva and looked at Jen. "Meredith was put on trial because we couldn't return her to her place of jurisdiction. If we can get her back home, our conviction is invalid. At least, that's the point I would make to the Judge Henshaw, who might be more receptive now that her daughters aren't being threatened to be turned to pulp by robots."

Jen nodded. Internally, Oscar said, "He's right there, Jen. This is really our Earth's problem."

"Maybe," said Jen both internally and externally.

Finally, Geneva said, "I understand your passion and feelings, Jennifer. But you haven't been back home. Meredith's situation is less important than *millions* of people losing their souls, and we almost certainly need her help to get back."

"She's lost most of her powers," said Jen quickly.

Geneva shook her head. "You don't lose channeling powers like hers, Jen. Most likely, she's lost her ability to fully access them due to the coma. And, well, given your attitude, she probably has a lot more power than you think and just hasn't let you know. I can probably channel with her and infuse some probability cloud particles and jump start them, kind of like jump starting the battery of a car that's been idle for months."

"I'm not sure about that. Even so, that might not get us back."

"I do think we need to use *Mars* as the transition point," said Geneva thoughtfully. "It's much more parallel across the dimensions right now than Earth. But regardless, we need Meredith."

"I'm not . . . she may not help," said Jen. "We obviously don't get along."

Geneva set a glare at Jen and said evenly but firmly, "She is my friend, and I *expect* to see her no later than tomorrow. Is that *clear*?"

Jen wasn't going to get into a face down with Geneva. She said evenly, "Very well."

"I need to file my motion with the judge," said Colin quickly. "Getting her released is going to be essential to working with her. We can't portal out of the prison."

"Fine. Get it done."

Then Jen turned to leave.

Geneva tried to stop her, putting up a hand and saying, "Let's talk, Jen."

"Colin will set you up in a room," said Jen bluntly as she stormed out.

Geneva looked at Colin. "She is upset beyond anything I ever saw."

Colin nodded. "Some of that is probably the news about Sheila Warren. They had been friends since Jen was a child."

"I know," said Geneva sadly.

"But . . . her feelings about Meredith are as hard as stone. It grates on her."

Geneva shook her head and said softly, "I wasn't kidding about Hell, Colin. It . . . sometimes, you have to be in a situation to truly understand it. I would hope I would never torture Necra the way Meredith did. But when I am honest about it . . . I can't say that I wouldn't. I *hope* I wouldn't. But I don't *know* that I wouldn't. So how can I condemn my friend?"

"You can't . . . you *are* Meredith's friend, so I will betray a confidence. This is our secret."

"Understood."

"She has post-traumatic stress disorder and was under the influence of the repressed memory of being forced to drink the liquefied corpse of the guard whose trust she betrayed to sneak into Project Rift," said Colin firmly.

"My God," said Geneva, horrified. "How could anyone . . . I've heard of horrible things, Colin, seen horrible things. That . . . is the worst. By a wide margin."

Colin nodded. "I know I am right about this. I know she was not in control of her actions. I just couldn't *prove* it." He slammed a fist on the table and rose. "It is my greatest failure, Miss Kane, though I must point out the whole thing was rigged by Tremas and the robots and their master. Regardless, I can make up for it by getting her and you back to your home."

"I appreciate the help."

"Come. Let me show you to your room . . . and perhaps we can talk of happier things, like this ring on your finger."

She laughed. "Ah, noticed it, did you?"

"What's his name?" asked Colin with a sly smile.

"Lon. Yeah, let's talk about him."

Chapter Five
Release

"I thought you forgot about me," Meredith said to Colin as she stood outside the prison gate, wearing old jeans that fit a little tight, white sneakers, and a pink shirt with red squares, the latter a gift from Colin.

"Hardly, m'dear, but I am a man of many missions," he said, stepping out of a limo and smiling. He wore a silver suit with a red handkerchief, rose, and tie.

"You always visit at nine, not this morning. No word. I started to think fucking robots got you, then they hustle me to the warden, so then I think I'm going to get raped," she said. She'd been beaten and raped by a team of guards and robots in prison. "Then like, wham-bam, thank you, ma'am, I'm here at the gate and you roll up!"

"I can take you back inside if you're *that* annoyed by it," said Colin with a smile.

She laughed. "Do that and I'll shove an ice-pick up your ass! Where are we going? What's going on? Why are we in a limo?"

Colin said nothing. He got inside, and once Meredith was inside, he tapped the top of the luxurious limo and the driver moved away from the curb.

"Mystery pisses me off, Colin," said Meredith impatiently.

"Everything has changed. Someone has arrived — someone from *your* Earth."

Her eyes widened. "Well . . . fuck me good," she said. "Who?"

"Geneva Kane."

Meredith was stunned. "How the fuck is *that* possible?"

"You can't fucking be here, Kane. Stop cheating the laws of tachyonic and portal physics," said Meredith with a smile as she entered the conference room at the downtown Ops office.

"Meredith! Oh, my God!" shouted Geneva, and they hugged. And for once, Meredith enjoyed the hug.

They sat down and Geneva said, "We . . . we . . . the volcano exploded after . . . my God, Sam will be so happy."

She smiled. "He's okay?"

Geneva nodded, but sadly. "He took some time off. He's . . . he's not director anymore. There have been some changes, but Sam is doing fine. He's mostly working with Jameson."

"Oh," said Meredith, a little surprised Sam had stepped down. "Well, that's good. That old fucker Jameson will have a heart attack some day."

Geneva leaned in and said, "Hey, if we keep moving across dimensions, that old turd will outlive us all!"

Meredith laughed. "Could be."

Then Geneva said seriously, "Be that as it may, we face grave danger."

Geneva gave her backstory. Meredith listened attentively, then said, "Fucking Kelkirk and his fuck-face partners. Yeah, I can see them thinking killing millions to save billions is a good deal. Of course, they never make *themselves* one of the millions. They're always in the billions that get spared."

"Precisely."

"I'll do what I can. I've lost some power, but it's there. It might take time."

"It can't take long," said Geneva. "It's not like they do roll call on Mars. I mean, it's truly an inescapable prison. And our geometric spell had its own signature distortion, so if they are detecting channeling, they won't know about it that way. But eventually, inevitably, someone will notice I'm not there. And as soon as it's discovered I'm missing, all Hell will break loose."

"We forgot someone," said Karla, reviewing the notes from the last three days as she stood in the reception area of the main dining hall in the Martian prison in our dimension. Nearby, several people were playing cards. Seated at a round card table were Judge 1040EZ and 1040A, Ashley, and Thunder.

Karla Karlson glared. "Where's Geneva Kane?"

Karlson was one of the closest Consortium members to Calico Kelkirk. She was a busty, statuesque blonde with shoulder length hair usually kept in a bun on her head, bangs across the front. She wore mascara, pink lipstick, and a lot of pink blush, trying to hide the wrinkles on her skin. Her eyes were sky blue, and she was a native of Berlin, but she was perfectly fluent in English.

Now forty-two, she liked to dress as if she were half that age. Her waist had started to expand and her breasts sag, despite some augmentation. However, despite her desperate efforts to cling to a younger appearance, she was a pleasant person. Not a talker, more a doer.

Like any TM, Karla had the ability to use a glamour to modify her appearance. She could make herself appear older or younger, modeled on her genetic structure, which was keyed to her aura. But she wasn't doing that at the moment. She was doing a weekly check on the Martian prison. Before Kelkirk died, Calico usually handled this chore. Now that she was busy with the master plan to save humanity, this duty was taken up by Karla.

The assistant was an old man named Albert who looked like a beleaguered butler. Adjusting his glasses, he checked the roster on the top of the clipboard, which had the notes Karla had been reviewing.

Then he looked up. "Uh, she's been sick in her room."

Karla's eyes narrowed. "I'll check. What room?"

"Building 14, room 46."

Karla exited, noticed by Thunder, who kept checking his cards and smoking his cigarette, blatantly ignoring the multiple signs on the wall.

When she was gone, he put his cards in the pot and said, "Three, and Crickey, team, I think the old shit has hit the fan, as you Americans say."

Ashley said, "Blondie, you mean?"

"Yup. Looking for Geneva."

Ashley nodded. Both judges turned white and looked at each other. Then 1040A said, "I'll fold."

"I bet you will," said Ashley dryly. Then she shoved in some chips and said, "Ante up, boys. This could be the last round."

"We'll see," said Thunder.

Moments later, Karla returned. She walked haughtily to their table and stood between the judges, putting a hand on each shoulder respectively. As she did this, she whispered, "Where is Kane?"

Thunder looked up. "She's been puking and shittin' her daks, so she's in her room."

Karla met his gaze, then she looked at Ashley. "Where is she?"

"In her room," said Ashley.

"I just went there. She hasn't been in there in at least two days."

Thunder shrugged and smiled. "I guess we aren't that close of friends."

Karla increased the pressure on the judges' shoulders. "I want to know where she is, and if not, I'll be glad to introduce you to the torture devices we have here for troublesome prisoners."

"T-t-t-t-torture?" squeaked 1040A.

Thunder snorted. "We tried to escape. It was a portal. It failed, I would assume. She vanished an' we ain't seen her since."

Karla studied him. "You don't seem to upset."

"She's just another Sheila," he said.

Ashley added, "It was a million to one shot. It was her idea. She took the risk. The rest of us are quite happy to keep playing cards here."

Karla snorted. "I doubt that. But I do believe you. Kane was opposed to Calico, according to her. She would be foolish enough to throw away her life on a suicidal escape plan."

She stormed away and radioed the news to Calico. They both assumed the shift had killed Geneva. There was no trace of her aura signature on Earth, and portaling from Mars to Earth was about as likely as a worm figuring out the law of thermodynamics.

Back at the table, Ashley said to Thunder, "She seems satisfied."

Thunder shrugged. "They probably figure she's dead."

"She probably is," said Ashley sadly. Then she looked at 1040A. "I knew you'd fold."

"Oh, shut up."

Chapter Six
Radar
Wednesday, 5/27/20

"I thought you guys forgot about me," said the human shaped robotic version of John Patience, who generally went by the handle Radar the next morning, Wednesday the twenty-seventh. The wind caused his curls to dance. His smile was clearly a smirk.

"My dear old chap, don't go all emo on me, as the kids say today," said Colin, walking up a worn trail from his parked, military Jeep. They were in an Arizona desert cave north of Yuma, a small town of about eighty thousand at the border of California, Arizona, and Mexico. They weren't far from railroad tracks, but there were no trains. The desert was windy, a late-season cold front sweeping through. The time was around nine in the morning.

Radar laughed. "If there's one thing I ain't, Brit-boy, it's emo."

Colin gestured, so the three ladies exited the jeep. Geneva and Jen exited the jeep first, wind blowing her hair. She wore a red sweater vest over a white, long-sleeved shirt, gray pants that hugged her perfect hips perfectly, and white, over-the-knee length boots. Jen wore a white shirt, a yellow windbreaker, and white pants, offset by black sneakers. Meredith hung back, finishing a game on her phone. She wore a royal blue headband, a white and green striped, short-sleeved shirt, frayed jeans, and black booties.

"Hi, Jen," said Radar. Jen nodded, then Radar looked at Geneva. "So *you're* Geneva Kane," said John with a smile.

Geneva studied him. He was tall, well over six feet, and gaunt with curly gray hair, a very weathered face, a thick mustache, and haunted blue eyes. Probably in his early fifties, but in good shape . . . well, of course, were he human he would've been in good shape.

Interestingly, his aura radiated paranormal, but she sensed something else odd about him. Discreetly, she used an aura detection spell while Jen introduced Colin and Meredith to him.

Finally, Geneva stepped forward. "You're interesting."

"Glad you think so, Kane."

"You know me?" she asked in surprise.

Radar smiled, amused by her suspicion. "I'm a seer, which I assume the crew here told you about. I knew your *parallel* self, but she died a while back. Knew of her, anyhow. On your world, which is our world, I met your grandfather once at a comic convention."

Geneva put one hand on a hip and smiled. "Really? He rarely attended them. They were a distraction from his work."

"He was at Chicago Con in '86. Trust me."

Geneva laughed. "He was indeed. Did you talk to him?"

"Briefly. Nice old guy. But enough about him." Radar clapped his hands. "C'mere, ol' niece of mine."

He and Meredith hugged.

Geneva looked at Colin. "He's a robot."

"Yes. He has several robotic bodies, but none of the human robots are real. His real body is a gold-plated thing that makes him look like a science-fiction robot."

Geneva just looked at him. "How did all *that* happen?"

Radar interrupted. "Zenith. To make a long, painful story short, after she came after my brother's family, Meredith's parents . . . I went after her. To say I got my ass-kicked is like saying World War II was a little tiff. Basically, she killed my ass, and I only survived here by getting my body and brain shoved into a big gold robot that makes me look like either a fancy vacuum cleaner or an old Oldsmobile."

"You're kidding," said Geneva.

"Nah, he's not, but it's not important," said Meredith. She turned to her uncle. "What do you think?"

Colin looked at them, all expectant. He hesitated. Then he looked at Jen, "You realize this likely would be a one-way trip. Is this world safe without you?"

"I believe so. Besides Joshua, Nile, and Kahlia, I have a couple other trusted agents in key areas," said Jen, parroting words fed to her by Oscar.

"Look, not to brag, but I'll be going in my real, uh, gold-plated body. The six robotic bodies, including this one, that run around here can stay, and they'll function pretty well even without my core consciousness."

"What do you mean?" asked Jen, sensing confusion from both Anissa and Oscar as well.

"Well, we're like a network. I can move my own consciousness in and out of all seven bodies at will. But the other robots don't generally go inert, unless I order it. They still obey instructions. They can't channel like me, but if you need to take out a low-level TM, they can punch with the best of them."

Jen nodded. "Not exactly the concern I had, but it's good they'll be around. They'll be okay."

"Okay. Good." Radar rubbed his chin. "I've been researching ever since the kid here popped up in the hospital. There's a way to get back to Jen Earth with geometric channeling, putting Meredith in the center. But it wouldn't work without the unique tachyons of the probability cloud." He looked at Jen. "I thought at first you could provide that, but your aura isn't quite right. Because you're a 'soul' survivor, it behaves slightly differently than hers," he said, pointing at Geneva.

"The cloud helps direct the portal?" asked Geneva.

"It gives us a chance. This is a nearly impossible task, but using the PC tachyons infused in your body, well, we have like a thirty-five percent chance. One in three."

"Better than the odds I made it here alive in the first place," said Geneva.

"What precisely do we do?" asked Colin.

Radar put his hands on his hips and bit his lip. "It's a dual square with whoever is going back in the inside square and Meredith in the middle. The idea situation is this," he said, using a stick to draw in the sand. "The outer square is four of my six robot bodies. They can handle the spell because I can leave a small part of my consciousness in them. Inside that robotic square is another square with Colin, the original and gold version of me, Jen, and Geneva, and Meredith in the middle of that inner square. That focuses all the tachyonic particles on Meredith in a double geometric fashion. Because of the focus on Quotient, we should come up somewhere within a mile or two of him. Can't get it any closer than that."

Geneva frowned. "This is a complex spell. Can the robots and, no offense, Colin handle it?"

Radar nodded. "Yeah. Don't forget, you and Jen have probability cloud exposure, those particles in your aura. That increases our odds. And Meredith is the one taking the brunt of the energy."

Everyone stared at the drawing. Finally, Meredith looked at her uncle. "What if it goes wrong?"

"Well . . . none of us will ever know it. We'll be disseminated at a molecular level through a myriad of dimensions. Well . . . other than you, niece. For you, it will be like having your skin scraped off with a potato peeler and mixed with Drain-o. Still up for it?"

She laughed. "That's not even in my top ten of pain. Yeah, I'm up for it. When?"

"Now," said Geneva. "We can't wait. Every delay gives them a chance to implement their plan."

Radar added, "From everything I see, she's right. I see nothing after today. That means we gotta change that, which means today is likely the last chance. My other robot bodies and my real self are inside the cave." He thumbed over his shoulder.

Jen looked at Colin. "Well?"

Colin shrugged. "There's no time like the present to die. I'm just worried if this Quotient entity is so powerful, can we stop him if this ridiculous plan *does* work and we do get where we're going?"

"Shit, Colin, you've got me, Geneva Kane, Unc here, and Jen Saunders. The three of us are the most powerful people in existence. If we can't get it done, then it ain't gonna get done," said Meredith confidently.

Colin clapped his hands. "Then let's get started."

"Done," said Jen, marking the last point of the exterior square in the sand nearly two hours later.

"Then let's get into position," said Geneva, quickly taking charge.

The team said little, realizing the gravity of the situation. They were also working feverishly, for the spell had to be precise or it would simply rip them apart. Geometric spells that broke containment were usually catastrophic to the user; death or serious injury was virtually guaranteed.

When they were finished, the real robot, the gold version, emerged from the cave. Geneva was astonished.

"Wow. You are . . . whoa."

"Thanks, kid," he said, the voice in his 'true' form a bit more electronic than the version that had been chatting with them since arrival.

The true Radar was glistening gold in color, about six feet tall, with a very round head and a torso shaped like a pot belly stove. Extendable tentacles that looked like metal vacuum cleaner hoses connected the torso to metal hands and feet that looked like part of a child's toy more than a sophisticated machine. The robot was compact and buxom, like an offensive tackle, in the head and torso, but the arms and legs were thin and skinny. The fact that it didn't tip over was amazing. And it had no neck.

Geneva looked at Colin. "You get up to some strange business in this dimension."

"Bah, this is nothing compared to the bloody blue movie district in London," he said with a mock pout.

The gold Radar said to Jen, "You should have someone from Ops come up here and check on my other four selves post-spell. I'm not sure what the effect will be on them."

"I've called Joshua. Kahlia is on the way. She was on assignment in Palm Springs."

"Good."

They all looked at each other.

Geneva finally spoke. "I know we could all die doing this, but I do not believe we will." She balled her fists and looked down at them, as if she were Supergirl about to punch a planet. Then she looked at each of them in order as she spoke.

"You are all my friends. I love you all, and I am honored to fight by your side. But the real battle isn't making it back. The real battle is against Quotient when we get there." Then her voice rose. "We will get back. I fought back from Hell. I do not lose when the stakes are high."

"None of do," said Meredith.

Then Meredith put a hand on Radar's gold shoulder. "Unc, it's really in your ball court now."

He nodded. "Into position everyone."

The tension was incredibly high.

Inside Jen, Anissa said internally to Oscar, "What's the real risk, doc?"

"For you, very high if you call me doc again!" Then seriously he said, "We are essentially walking naked into a thunderstorm in the forest hoping not to get struck by lightning. At any point, the spell could invert or the tachyonic force could escape the spell. Our only real advantage are the four robot Radars on the outside square. They have much more stamina than a normal human."

"Could this . . . doc, could this really be it?"

"I don't know."

Anissa was quiet for a minute. Then she said, "We should take care of Jen's alters."

"No. Jen is, well, a daughter to me, Anissa. I'll stay with her. You go be a nurse and care for the children."

"Got it . . . good luck, doc."

"And you."

The fact that he didn't chew her out for calling him doc again left her *very* worried.

Outside, everyone was in position. As they assembled, Radar said to his niece, "Unfortunately, Meredith, this is going to hurt like a motherfucker."

She looked at him. "If there's one thing I've learned in my life, it's how to take pain. I'll manage."

Radar looked around. "Anyone gotta pee before we go?"

No one laughed.

"Fine. Any last comments?"

Geneva said. "No. I've prayed for us all. We're ready."

"Fine. We start on five . . . four . . . three . . . two . . . one."

For ten seconds nothing happened.

Then psychic heat began to rise from the inner square, creating a haze of yellow and the smell of smoke in the area.

Meredith screamed a wretched, agonizing scream, the cry of the damned.

And then they were gone.

Chapter Seven
Rude Awakening

Slowwwwwwwwwwwly, Geneva opened her eyes.

Immediately, she saw blue through a white haze, heard the crashing of waves, and felt heat.

Instantly alert, she rolled over and shouted, "We did it!"

Then she shut up, realizing she was alone. Now on her left side, she was looking at the most gorgeous ocean she had ever seen. The water was a blue-green color usually seen only on advertisements of vacation islands, images she used to see during long Maine winters on commercials from travel companies.

Sand coated her back and left side. She was tired, but able to move. Quickly, she got to her feet and as she brushed off as much sand as she could, looked around for her partners.

But she was alone.

"Weird," she said.

Now the ocean was to her right. She stood on a sandy, white-brown layer of beach that was about as wide as a football field, approximately fifty yards. Past that was an extremely dense thicket of brush: palm trees, bushes about six feet tall, and vines and other twisting plants cutting out all light inside. It was like a solid wall of vegetation.

Ahead, the shore curved back to the left. The undergrowth looked thick, so she decided to walk up the shore and see if it thinned out. Pausing before she left, she noticed an odd purple and yellow stain on the sand. She also realized she was bleeding from the nose. But it had almost stopped.

Pausing for thirty seconds to pinch her nose, she studied the island. When she finally staunched the bleeding, she put her hands on her hips and looked at the lovely water. She approached and tested it. Salt water.

"Great. I have the ultimate beach paradise and everything I need . . . except food and water."

Moving ahead, she wondered why she had been separated from the team. It seemed like early morning. Was it the same day? Probably. She wasn't hungry, and she didn't even have to pee.

No, they couldn't have been separated long. Were they dead? They wouldn't have forgotten her, wouldn't have left her behind. There were no human footprints on the shore — obviously there were birds and crabs active in the area — so what had happened? This was the problem with using the probability cloud. Prediction was impossible.

After eight minutes of walking, she heard noise in the undergrowth. Turning and preparing to battle, she relaxed and shouted with a glee worthy of a sorority girl as Jen Saunders emerged.

"We've been looking for you! Thank goodness!" said Jen, rushing over to her friend.

"Is everyone else okay?"

"Yes! We all landed in slightly different spots. Also, we haven't got Radar with us. Colin has a device that says Radar was diverted into the ocean a few hundred miles away. We don't know why. Possibly his metal body skewed the portal a bit."

"I hope he doesn't rust," said Geneva.

"He should be fine. He can convert into a flotation device. But it will take a while to get back here. Let me signal the others."

Geneva waited, enjoying the sun on her face, the crash of the waves, the sand on her body. As spectacular as Mars had been . . . inside, it was just a hotel. There was nothing like this feeling, the feeling of weather and earth — especially for an elemental channeler.

The others arrived. After a few seconds of relief and back-slapping, Geneva said, "Any ideas where we are?"

Colin studied his phone. "I'm assuming the geography is relative stable in quantitative relationship to our world, which puts us somewhere in the Pacific, between Hawaii and Japan, closer to Hawaii."

"The middle of no-fucking-where," said Meredith.

"Let's try and find civilization. We'll need water," said Jen.

"Agreed," said Geneva.

Jen and Geneva walked together, towards the middle of the beach, while Colin and Meredith were to their right. Meredith kept a wide berth from Jen.

"Perhaps we'll find some topless girls with leis," said Colin.

Geneva said, "I'm a little worried. Why would we wind up in nowhere? We're supposed to wind up within a mile of Quotient."

"Unc might have blown it," said Meredith. "That wasn't supposed to happen. And he got blown hundreds of miles away. Maybe *he* wound up near Quotient."

"Assuming he told us the entire truth," said Colin grimly.

Meredith snapped, "What does *that* mean?"

Colin was taken aback by her anger, and quickly said, "Oh, no offense, m'dear, none. It's just that, well, he's a seer, Meredith. It may well be he knew that this would happen and had to hide that fact from us."

She looked shocked. "He wouldn't lie to me."

"Sins of omission," said Colin.

"It doesn't matter," said Jen. "Be alert. Just because it looks quiet doesn't mean it is."

Geneva said to the group, "How does everyone feel? Can everyone feel their auras, channel?"

"I'm good," said Jen, then to Meredith she tentatively asked, "Uh, are you okay? You did all the heavy lifting on our portal, so to speak."

"I'm starting to . . . tingle," she said thoughtfully. "And fast. It's almost like . . . I'm supercharging. It's weird. It must be some side effect of the portal. I feel a bit hot, like I got a really bad sunburn. But I'm charging fast, though it will still take time."

Geneva nodded. "I feel the same. Maybe it's being back in touch with our native Earth."

Meredith just shrugged.

Suddenly, Colin said, "There's a path through the brush."

Gesturing, he urgently signaled the others to follow him. They did so. After they followed the trail for about half a mile and reached the end, the brush ended, and all were shocked by the sight below them.

They now realized they were on a ridge far above a valley on an island that was lushly green and mountainous. Despite the morning sun on the beach, there were clouds covering the peaks of some of the mountains in the distance.

But that wasn't the *surprising* sight. The surprise was that below their vantage point was a mansion with a huge driveway. The main house was surrounded by a huge white wall capped with orange tile, and there was a medieval gate that swung open for vehicles. Once it had been a hotel for military guests, a white and orange building with turrets and towers, looking Oriental more than American. Inside had been a huge, grassy courtyard on which several big dogs like Dobermans and bloodhounds had run wild, but that was now completely submerged under ocean water.

A battered American flag flew proudly over the awning over the front entrance, still as originally designed with double-doors typical of a large hotel. Water had covered the grounds right up to the door, but the house itself appeared undamaged, as was a small concrete walkway leading to the wide driveway, which was slightly elevated and not underwater. Near the house in the middle of the driveway was a large black box made of plywood that was about ten by ten feet.

Geneva turned to Meredith. "My God! I think I've seen this place in the files! *Is this place Mort's house?*"

Meredith's eyes widened in shock. "Holy fuck! I think it is! Storm Island!"

"What's a Mort's house?" asked Colin. "And a Storm Island? Some drug runner's home?"

Geneva quickly shook her head. "No. It's a place owned by this guy named Mort that Searly and Clarke Kent, bless him, ran into like a decade ago when they were undercover searching for this TM named Bill Montgomery in Hawaii. Mort was working with Nile Neferates. All he wanted was to help the homeless in Honolulu by turning them into zombies."[3]

Colin snorted. "Rather misguided."

Geneva nodded. "Yes. But this island is a tiny place, smaller than Guam. It basically was used in World War II and Vietnam as a military stopover, but it looks like its slowly sinking. I bet there's not more than ten square miles of land on this place."

Meredith said, "I remember Searly talking about this now. Sam said that Ops had jurisdiction, but they just gave it back to the military to see if they could make any use of it."

"This place was all but forgotten, I'd guess," said Geneva thoughtfully. "I mean, it's in the middle of nowhere in the Pacific, is smaller than a postage stamp, and has only a few dozen square miles of salvageable space."

"The island the world forgot," said Colin, rubbing his chin.

Meredith added, "For good reason. Anyhow, fuck that. The house is clearly not flooded. This would be the only building on the fucking place, so this has to be the spot. What the fuck is in that box on the driveway?"

"It's more like a storage bin than a box," said Jen, reflecting a thought by Anissa. Before she could elaborate, she was interrupted.

"Someone's coming out," said Colin, pointing dramatically.

Geneva gasped, so everyone else fell silent. Walking out of the mansion were Calico, the late TM Kelkirk's daughter, and her right-hand-man, Englehart.

Quickly, Geneva said with wide eyes, "Be ready for anything."

---

[3] See TM 1.8 "Just One of the Guys"

Thirty-one-year-old Calico Kelkirk strode quickly out of the house. She had chestnut brown hair, long and straight, parted in the middle. Her eyes were blue and narrow. Her face was thin, and her body was very thin except for a clearly artificially enhanced chest. She spoke in a clearly American accent — fitting as she was from the Detroit area before moving to Germany as a teenager.

She said to Englehart, "At least it's not raining."

"Indeed," said John Englehart, who was most often addressed by his last name as he despised the name John. Now sixty-one, Englehart was as energetic as he had been as a young man. Most of that was due a brutal schedule that involved balancing time between the Consortium and running his own Hollywood action show, *Fire Johnson At Large*, now in its fifth season. He was a large man, now weighing a solid 270 as he was overweight, but also tall at six feet and four inches. With a curly blonde beard and blond hair that showed only the smallest signs of aging, he looked much younger. Stylish glasses helped him appear bookwormish and inquisitive . . . accurate traits, but ones that hid a strong urge to save the world

Calico wore a black camisole and white pants, while Englehart wore white shorts and a black and yellow, flowered Hawaiian shirt and a straw hat. Calico wore cute black booties, while Englehart wore well-worn sandals. They walked the path from the main door to the driveway, which was slightly elevated and thus above the water. They were using chalk and a ruler started marking a hexagon, leaving the black storage box in the center.

"Something's going on," said Jen. "Those are clearly markings for geometric magic. This could be a portal — the water could be a cooling aid. We should stop them now."

Geneva put out her hand. "No, not yet. I don't see Quotient. I wish we could hear them."

Colin pulled a transmitter the size of a fly out of his pocket. "We can. I just need a slight gust of wind to guide my little bug down to the valley. Ops in our world is far more advanced than you savages here."

"I'll handle that," said Geneva. With that, a gentle gust of wind lifted the transmitter and sent it below.

"You're always so handy, Colin," said Jen with a smile.

Colin winked. "Let's listen."

They had to wait a moment for Geneva to guide the transmitter into place. Once it did, they could hear clearly.

For several minutes, Calico and Englehart simply used a laser rule and called out measurements. When they were done, there was a blue chalk hexagon with an 'X' marking each standing point.

"Why use a hexagon?" Colin asked Geneva.

"I don't know. Squares are the most powerful."

Once Calico marked the last X on the ground, she flipped the blue chalk up in the air like a wand and caught it. "Done. I think Karla should bring out Quotient first."

Geneva gasped. The others looked at her. And all of them saw something in her pretty eyes they had rarely — or maybe never — seen before.

Fear.

She started to tremble, but hid it. To Jen, she said, "We . . . we have to be careful. We could lose our souls."

"I know," said Oscar through Jen. "We'll handle it."

"Relax. I can zap our asses out of here if it gets hot," said Meredith.

Colin put a comforting hand on Geneva's shoulder, but she shrugged it off and said, "I don't need comfort. We need action."

"Not yet. There's more douche-bags coming out," said Meredith, pointing at the mansion.

She was right. Four more figures emerged. Two were known to Ops. Two were not.

The unknown people appeared to be a couple, as they were close to each other and holding hands. One was a picturesque platinum blonde with long, straight hair, pink lips, and brown eyes. Her face was full of freckles. The other was a tall black man who was prematurely half-bald and had the physique of a basketball player who retired and went on an eating binge — tall and wide. The blonde wore a pink camisole with jeans shorts, no shoes. The black man wore no shirt and white shorts with dirty white sneakers. Both appeared to be in their twenties, which they were.

"Who are they?" Meredith asked Geneva.

"No idea."

"This is maybe a stretch, but they do look familiar," said Jen thoughtfully. "In our dimension, the parallel world that is, when we were battling Zenith's acolytes when she still held control of the planet, we fought a couple that looked like these two — except the girl was fat and the guy skinny."

"I remember them. Yellow Gentry and Smith Pickrose," said Colin, snapping his fingers and clearly pleased at his recall.

"Yes. They could be them. They were from the Pacific Northwest, Oregon or somewhere with a lot of trees . . . they vanished after Joshua and I did the rewrite."

"More likely they simply had a history where they never became TMs," corrected Colin.

"True."

As if on cue, the woman turned to the man and said, "I'm nervous about this."

He patted her shoulder gently and said, "Me, too. But don't turn Yellow."

She rolled her eyes at the infantile pun. "Be serious. We're in a major league paranormal stuff here. Now that we're here, I'm worried we can't pull it off."

"We can't. But Calico can."

But while Jen and Colin were struck by Yellow and Smith, the other two caught Geneva's attention. Once was Karla, wearing a black blouse, gold belt, and black slacks.

The other was Nile Neferates.

Nile caught Meredith's attention as well, based on the glare Geneva saw on her blonde partner's face. Discreetly, Geneva put out a hand on Meredith's leg to calm her.

Neferates was now thirty-seven. She had long, dark hair parted in the middle, hair that was very curly and wavy at the end. Her eyes were dark, and she had the complexion of an Egyptian woman. Her forehead was large and shiny, and she was tall. Her breasts were attractive, artificially enhanced but not over the top. Presently, she wore a black sports bra and black yoga pants with white sneakers. She looked a bit hung over, or maybe worried.

In fact, all six of the people below looked *very* serious.

"We need a plan to take on all of them," said Geneva quickly. "Surprise is our only advantage."

"Hold hard for a moment," said Colin. "What are they up to?"

"My question as well," said Jen, parroting internal words from Oscar.

Using the bug, they listened in, but the six said nothing, instead moving towards clearly pre-arranged spots on the hexagon. The hexagon was about as wide as a big two-car garage, maybe 1,000 square feet, extending to the edge of the driveway.

Calico was clearly in charge, because everyone was looking back at her and waiting on her to settle her position before speaking. While she did this, Englehart and Nile channeled, drawing water from the flooded areas around the mansion towards the hexagon. Once the driveway was soaked in a few inches of water, they channeled earth to sink and hold it there.

Above, this wasn't unnoticed by the group. Colin said, "This *is* a portal exercise, the water to cool."

"But to do what?" added Geneva.

Jen said, "Hush. I think Calico is about to speak."

Through the bug, the others heard a lot of insect and bird noises, and the crashing of the waves. Were they listening, for example, from a hotel room, it would sound like a glorious tropical island.

But they weren't.

They were listening to a woman . . . a very determined woman convinced she was right.

Finally, Calico looked at her team and spoke. "We all understand the gravity of this operation. Many will die today, sacrificed for the greater good. I regret this, but we all know it is necessary. Quotient's success today will set the stage, to finalize my father's dream and save humanity." She looked at each one of them for several seconds and said, "I will not think any less of you should you back down now. You have all won my respect and . . . and love for your dedication helping me and my father and Englehart save humanity. There is great risk in this operation, risk of death and . . . and far worse. But I believe it the only way, as I hope do all of you. Will you all stand with me?"

Karla spoke immediately. "Of course."

The blonde and black man both nodded and the man said, "We're in."

Nile looked nervous, but she said, "We'll win."

Calico didn't even look at Englehart. She knew where he stood.

"Then we begin."

Reaching into her pocket, Calico used a remote control and the lid for the black box slid back. Because the Ops team was on the hill, they were able to look down and observe that there were five people inside the black box, arms stretched over their heads. They were on what looked like a wooden bed mattress, but a very sturdy one. They each had wrists bound to the upper bar and ankles bound to the lower bar. A central bar ran under them, across their backs for support. All five were nude and gagged with ball gags.

Geneva recognized them instantly.

"God, no!" she gasped. "It's Crystal, Thunder, Ashley, and the Judges! They helped me escape Mars." Looking at Colin she said wide-eyed, "She must be sacrificing them as punishment for helping me escape!"

Below, Englehart said to Calico, "We're ready, Calico."

"Then let us summon our partner."

With that, Karla spoke into her phone and said, "&^*&^*."

A yellow blur began to appear in the middle of the hexagon, about ten feet above the center.

Above them on the cliff's edge, Geneva heard this. Immediately, her eyes widened and her jaw literally fell.

"Oh . . . oh, *my God,*" she gasped.

They all looked at her in alarm, knowing something was wrong.

In panic, a state the others had never seen here, Geneva grabbed Meredith's and Colin's arms and hissed in a loud whisper, "They're doing it *now*! Don't you get it?!?! They're going to sacrifice my friends to create a portal and sacrifice all people they can to Quotient to generate the energy to get to Mars now! *We've got to stop them*!"

"We need a plan!" said Colin.

"There's no time," said Meredith. "There's only one way to stop them in time. The rest of you, start moving. I'm going down."

"Meredith, *wait*!" shouted Colin, reaching for her.

But she was gone.

Chapter Eight
Battle for the Fate of the World

The battle for the fate of the world on the island the world had forgotten was fast and brief, though complex.

Meredith knew it was impossible to rescue the hostages and stop the portal with six TMs circling her.

She had to disrupt the spell, and if the hostages died, they died.

Of all the team, she was the only one ethically and psychologically able to make that decision, and most importantly she was the only one able to instantly appear on the battlefield.

Taking the matter into her own hands, she portaled below and suddenly appeared before Nile Neferates.

The appearance of Meredith shocked everyone, but *particularly* Nile, for she had one terrible, *terrible* fear. During her time as a TM serving as an acolyte for Quafara, she had seen Meredith skewer Nile's friend, the TM Jill Tifton, on an ice pick. It was that act that made Nile rethink her, ah, career plans.

Fleeing Atlantia, she had been found by Kelkirk and given a role and a purpose with the Consortium. As a child, Nile had survived a gang rape, an act that had turned her against people and triggered her ability to channel. But with the Consortium, she had matured, and had found perhaps a simpler way to power and, more critically, safety.

That ended in a split second.

Meredith appeared and slashed out with her right hand, creating a knife of ice as she did so.

She slashed Nile's throat to the bone, spraying blood everywhere and pitching Nile backwards, dying as she fell.

This took a fraction of a second. During that time, the geometric channeling destabilized, as Nile lost position. Englehart screamed and quickly shut down the channeling, barely able to do so. He probably only managed to salvage the operation because Quotient was ultra-powerful and he . . . it? . . . continued to materialize — clearly his presence was due to the commands of Karla, *not* part of whatever ritual the other six were performing.

Calico acted the quickest and with aggressive and lethal force. A Kelkirk and a person highly focused on preparation, she had not taken for granted that working on the isolation of Storm Island and with everything in their control nothing could go wrong. Unlike the others, she was ready to act instantly. She spun to her left and picked up via TK four iron fence posts that had spikes on the top, part of a four-foot metal fence around a garden.

She hurled the rods at Meredith like spears.

Two facts doomed Meredith as the spears raced at her. First, the others were too far away to channel her into position faster than Calico could push the spears via telekinesis. Second, she was a bit slow in her reactions, having spent the past two years either in a coma or sitting in prison.

"Urkkkkkkkkkkkkkk!" she gasped as she was skewered through her abdomen in four directions by the spikes. They were heavy metal and propelled hard by Calico.

Meredith's guts flew everywhere, painting the water red, and she collapsed, stumbling forward and landing on Nile's corpse.

They were both dead.

This took 1.2 seconds.

Above, Geneva acted instantly, crying as she channeled, knowing Meredith was on a suicide mission. But she had to save the Martian Ops team. She channeled the water and wind to create a tidal wave to sweep the black box out of the hexagon. The spell was disrupted and chaos ensued, the five hostages were washed and blown up the stairs to crash into the house.

It was a rough ride for them, but the crash broke the wooden supports, and they quickly began to free themselves.

The rest of the team on the hill was moving downhill, covered by the fiercely gusting wind, driving water at the hexagon, blinding everyone.

Yellow and Smith instantly fled, running for the safety of the mansion.

Karla started using the rest of the fence spikes as spears, throwing them via TK randomly at the hillside, figuring that's where the attack had to come from. Then she turned to Quotient, who had fully materialized.

He looked strangely like yellowish Play-dough, the yellowish Play-dough seen in elementary schools across the country for decades. He vibrated and never seemed exactly the same size, varying from ten to twelve feet in diameter. He also seemed to be floating, hovering near the ceiling, about eight feet off the ground. The only feature was an eye, just a black dot, as if the ball where a lump of cookie dough with one huge chocolate chip in the middle . . . like a Hershey's Kisses' cookie. And the formation of the ball near the eye had a ridge that was an eyelid.

Karla and started shouting, sounding as if she were barking orders like a Gestapo officer. "@%@#! Down! ##$^! *&*&*. !"

Englehart moved to cover Calico, always his primary objective in any battle. He shouted to her, "How many?"

"The aura detectors pick up three — two now," she said, checking her phone, unaware Colin wasn't being picked up as he wasn't paranormal. Her face was splattered with blood, both Nile and Meredith's.

This occupied one side of the hexagon. With the death of Nile, the hexagon shape was disrupted, and steam began to rise from the water, which was now no longer the beautiful blue of the ocean but mixed with the red blood of Nile and Meredith.

On the opposite side of the hexagon, Yellow and Smith raced for the mansion. Yellow channeled water away from them as they raced up the driveway, while behind them Smith channeled earth, ripping up the driveway and providing some cover. He also tore up the far side of the mansion, the side mostly underwater and facing the cliff. Power poles and trees fell with it. They just barely avoided hitting the storage box holding the hostages — the impact had dislodged the judges, but not Ashley, Thunder, and Crystal. They were still freeing themselves. Yellow and Smith wanted escape, and instead of attacking merely ran around them and ducked into what they hoped was the security of the house.

Quotient had hesitated, but then acted under Calico's guidance and moved straight up, then swung away from Englehart and Calico. They remained on the bloody, wet driveway, which now was also hazy from steam and pretty much dry. The vaporization took only seconds once the hexagon was disrupted. They were desperately trying to contain the psychic heat. Normally, this would've been impossible, but as they had barely started the spell, they were able to manage it.

Meanwhile, Geneva and Jennifer raced down the hill. Their job was to stop Quotient. Geneva was gambling her probability cloud laced channeling would stop him, while Jen could cover her, for her aura was also lacked with PC tachyons.

Colin had a totem, a green gem, but no paranormal powers, so he knew he couldn't do anything against Calico, Englehart, and Karla except bleed on them. He raced for the house to help the Martian Ops team.

As Colin approached, Thunder channeled electricity from the house via an outside cable at the Yellow and Smith while shouting at Ashley, "Sheila, cover me! Crystal, house!"

To their left at the top of the driveway, Colin raced for the house, trying to help Crystal stop Yellow and Smith or find a weapon inside. His totem was about as useful as a water pistol in this kind of battle.

Crystal had never been a particularly strong channeler, and her imprisonment on Mars for such a long period of time had dulled her reflexes. As Sam Grant might say, she was like Michael Vick playing quarterback after his time in prison.

Smith began to channel earth through the doorway.

Crystal turned and tried to regain control of the earth from Smith. She managed to do that, controlling the area in front of her and Colin as he arrived to join her. But Yellow joined the battle, using TK to swing one of the dislodged utility poles from the initial landslide at Crystal.

This was a considerable feat, and clearly established Yellow as a premiere user of TM and TK. Most telekinetic users were like Jen Saunders, in that they were generally limited to roughly the ability to move with the mind what he or she could move physically. The pole had needed a crane to be set, and if Yellow were physically standing, she couldn't have rolled it over, let alone lifted it.

During this moment, Yellow was completely vulnerable. It took all of her concentration. Colin saw this, stopped running, and used his totem to raise a wave of water, which hadn't evaporated around the flooded areas of the mansion — it was not part of the channeling event and here it was several feet deep anyhow — driving the wave at Yellow, it approaching her from the right.

Crystal did not see the pole flying at her from behind. Nor did Colin, focused on Yellow.

Smith saw the action and covered Yellow, taking control of Colin's wave, wresting it from him and dissipating it.

The pole swung forward like a baseball bat.

Crystal was struck in the upper back. The impact caused a cracking sound like a tree coming down in a windstorm as her spine was shattered.

Yellow stopped channeling.

The pole simply dropped onto Crystal, driving her to the sandy ground.

But it didn't matter, because the impact had killed her already, shattering her spine. She died instantly.

Colin heard the scream from Crystal, who was now slightly behind him, but he didn't dare turn, because if he did Smith would have him.

Once Yellow won, she grabbed Smith and dragged him inside, slamming the door shut. The door was clearly a blast door, a large metal object not in place with the décor of the mansion. As Smith went, he gave a final push and a gigantic wave of sand and water ten feet tall raced at Colin.

"Oh, dear."

The wave hit Colin and drove him back and up the cliff, which now was a mess of damaged trees and brush mixed with mud.

He hit hard, and although he didn't quite lose consciousness, he was just barely conscious, unable to untangle himself from the mud, vines and branches in which he had been deposited.

On the driveway, Karla and Quotient had moved to the right, as if trying to make it to the bottom of the driveway. That wasn't Karla's objective. She was just trying to separate from Calico and Englehart, because Karla knew with Quotient she had no need for cover. She didn't want to be picked off in the battle while she was trying to guide Quotient's attack on Geneva and Saunders.

That left Ashley and Thunder to try and take down Calico and Englehart, who had finished dispersing the psychic heat. The judges simply ran away, taking cover around the side of the house.

"Crickey," said Thunder as he raced forward.

"WTF," said Ashley, and she began channeling wind. She was good at it and had a lot of power stored due to her weeks of imprisonment on Mars.

Calico shot Englehart a look and shouted, "Karla is okay. We've got to take these two."

"On it."

Ashley was running, but she stopped, the ground her rumbling like an upset stomach thanks to Smith's work at the mansion; the residual effect was felt on the driveway. Bracing herself, she channeled wind from the ocean for all she was worth.

A typhoon raced off the flooded lawn towards the combatants.

It flew past the point where Geneva and Jennifer were trying to corral Quotient and Karla and towards Calico.

Calico grimaced and braced herself, then took control of the wind. She had known the instant Meredith appeared they were in a battle for everything they had worked for, that Meredith would not have come alone and Ops would not back down. Tears rolled down her eyes as she fought.

But despite her sorrow, she *fought*.

Both women screamed as they fought for control of the typhoon. It was an agonizing effort, like running in quicksand.

Thunder was desperately looking for anything connected to electricity, having drained the relatively weak current of the house to fund their initial escape and blowback effort. He found an outlet near the fence, but it was dead. His unique channeling ability helped him sense electricity, but all he could detect was a generator deep in the mansion, which he activated via his power and drew upon.

Stuck on an island with little resources, Thunder was still roughly a match for his nearly equal aged combatant Englehart, who did not have the stamina for a prolonged battle.

"Struth, you're tough for an old codger," said Thunder as Englehart parried Thunder's attempt to channel earth and dislodge his foe.

"Age is in the mind," said Englehart. He desperately wanted to dispatch Thunder and help Calico. Hearing her scream had upset him. In all of their battles over the years, he had never heard that. And, of course, like Calico, he knew this was a battle for *everything*. He wasn't as sad as Calico. He had never believed they could sway anyone on Ops to their side, was more psychologically prepared for this battle.

Thunder had one huge advantage, that being his physical acumen. He was in superb shape, while Englehart was a Pillsbury dough boy. Thunder recognized this and used his channeling to set up a physical attack. He kept disrupting the ground under and around Englehart and kept moving closer, holding his electricity at bay until he was close enough to deliver a lethal strike that couldn't be parried.

For his part, Englehart just wanted Thunder out of the way. But Englehart had to defend the assault on his patch of land like a man stuck on an island in a sea of sharks. He knew if he went down, he was done. Furthermore, Ashley's cyclone had severely disrupted the wind and water in the area. Englehart couldn't grab much wind without disrupting his surrogate daughter's attempt to steal control of the cycle from Ashley. And Englehart couldn't use TM to hurl objects because the wind was too strong.

Thunder finally won. He broke through and used earth to rise and drive him into Englehart, the force allowing him to drive a devastating punch under Englehart's jaw.

Englehart wasn't a physical fighter. He took the full force of the punch. The sound was like a cement block dropping on concrete. Englehart's head pitched back, and he was out cold before he hit the ground.

But Calico was also winning. Her battle with Ashley became purely an arm-wrestling contest taken to the extreme. Ashley was at the peak of her power, while Calico had burned some setting up the ritual and stopping Meredith. But Calico clearly was the more powerful channeler, and she could also use TK via TM. While they wrestled the cyclone, Calico realized deception was her only hope. The two women fell to their hands and knees, the tornado of sand and water and plant debris swirling around them and creating a shriek that sounded like all the souls of Hell were coming to take them. It made speech impossible, not that either of them had anything to say to the other anyhow.

Ashley felt like she was winning. She was closing the circular cone behind Calico, getting within feet. If Ashley could somehow strike Calico with the wind, suck her into the cyclone, she had won. Her nose was bleeding, and she was shaking . . . but the same was happening to Calico.

Calico waited, a spider patiently letting the fly struggle to the bitter end. There was a rock about the size of a golf ball two feet to Calico's left, and the combatants were about ten yards across from each other.

Timing was everything.

Calico pulled a faint, something like a woman faking submission to a rapist, then trying to kick him in the balls. She fell to her right side and groaned and allowed Ashley to push the cyclone in about half a foot. The screaming was louder now for Calico.

Ashely was like a race car driver sensing weakness at the finish line, and she put the pedal to the medal, pushing the back of the cyclone for all she was worth. All her focus was on taking Calico down. She needed less than a second.

She didn't have it.

Using TK, Calico lifted the rock and hurled it into Ashley's face.

The impact caused Ashely to scream and fall back.

Calico wrested control of the cyclone.

Like that, it was over. Calico swept up Ashley in the cyclone and redirected it into the mansion.

As Calico took control of it, she snagged Thunder in the vortex.

"Crickey!" cried Thunder, realizing he had no chance. Like a quarterback suddenly surrounded by five blitzing linebackers, Thunder simply took a defensive position and rolled into a ball on the sand. Calico still swept him up and drove him into the far side of the mansion, a section that was still mostly underwater, a section she knew Yellow and Smith would not be inside.

"Calico," said Englehart, rushing to help her to her feet.

Breathing heavily, exhausted, Calico looked up at him. "I wet myself."

"Sorry. Come on."

They turned towards Karla and Quotient.

All they saw was a yellow haze, a fog so thick that all that was left were hazy shadows.

Those shadows were in mortal combat.

At this point, Calico looked in horror at Englehart. "What do we do?"

"Hope Karla and Quotient are winning," he said grimly. "We've got to cover them."

Calico nodded. Both of them were covered in sand and Calico's clothes were ripped by flying debris. Englehart's right side of his face was swollen like a boxer suffering a bad loss.

Noticing his face, Calico asked, "Are you okay?"

"I'm using a healing spell as we speak. I see Ridgeway. He's out up the hill."

"There's Ashley. A pole is on her — I think she's dead."

"I saw Yellow and Smith make it into the house. The door is still secure, so they should be safe. They've had enough time to set the charges to blow the place. Are there any other Ops agents?"

Calico shook her head. "No. I see who is here. How did Patience survive that battle years ago and wind up here today?"

Englehart looked at the yellow fog. "I assume she was never dead and was in that blank slate dimension we've heard so much about, especially given Saunders is here." He shook his head in surprise. "Somehow, Kane must have portaled there, and come back to Mars with Saunders and Meredith, and then they reached us and launched an attack. They didn't wait. Somehow, they knew what we were doing. But I don't know how."

Of course, Englehart and Calico had no clue of Radar's existence or involvement.

Calico nodded. "It doesn't matter right now." Then she looked at Englehart with regret. "I shouldn't have killed Patience. I just . . . . reacted."

"It's understandable," he said, putting a hand on her shoulder. "But I don't think Ops will see it that way."

Calico looked at the fog. "What can we do to help Karla?"

"We don't dare go in there. That's pure tachyon energy flowing around them. We'd have better luck crossing a World War I trench battlefield stark naked. We just cover them and hope our side comes out."

"And if not?"

"We fight to the death."

Chapter Nine
Battle for the Soul

Dying, Geneva Kane screamed.

While the battle raged outside the tachyon cone, the truly critical battle was occurring *inside* the cone, where Quotient was invading the mind and soul of Jennifer Saunders.

Or at least *attempting* to invade.

Inside the tachyon cone, there were really two battles happening. Geneva was terrified of Quotient, feeling a fear she had never felt in her life. This level of extreme fear was a new feeling for Geneva, one of the most resilient people in Ops, a very powerful woman. Yes, she had felt fear when Quafara threw her into Hurricane Saturday. Sure, she had felt fear when Gerald died while battling Doctor Voodoo in Atlantia. Hell, she had even felt fear the first day she channeled, when her old bloodhound, Lockshire, had nearly drowned in the ocean near Gerald's historical lighthouse home.

But this was different. Her faith in God and knowledge of the soul wasn't *abstract* to her but concrete fact, as real as the island on which she stood. All channelers knew the soul existed — they could read auras, which were the physical representation of the soul. Auras were fundamental to channeling, which in a primitive way was simply using soul energy to move objects. It was a primal type of paranormal activity.

The potential destruction of her soul almost paralyzed her with fear.

So she froze up when it was time to battle Quotient.

As she and Jen approached, Quotient used his powers to lift sand from the beach around them and mixed it with tachyon energy, effectively sealing them off from the rest of the battle.

Karla shouted, "(*&%*%^&!!"

Geneva turned her attention to Karla. If Karla were ordering Quotient, maybe they could control him if *she* were out of the picture.

Meanwhile, Jen braced herself and tried to use her TK to grab Quotient. Their initial belief as discussed during planning sessions on the parallel world quickly proved correct: Quotient *did* have mass, he wasn't intangible, and he was light. He was much like a big balloon.

So using TK, she grabbed him and tried to drag him down to the ground and pop him, so to speak.

But he fought back.

And then all of them screamed a ghastly scream that could have terrified the devil himself.

Inside Jen's mind, Quotient was suddenly the sun in the park that was used as the communion are and her safe place for her and her alters. The sky was yellow.

Jen stood up on the top of one of the picnic tables, which instead of being freshly painted bright red were now rotting wood covered in earwigs. Around her were her alters, Oscar, and Anissa. Instantly she recognized the problem and screamed in panic, "We're all here! Who's running our body?"

The answer was obviously — no one. Her physical body fell into a coma as she fought for her soul.

Jen screamed. All the alters, Jen, Oscar, and Anissa were all represented by their most primary representations, how they felt about themselves. All of them looked normal; Anissa wore jeans and a yellow shirt; Oscar wore a collared shirt and gray pants; Jen wore black pants and a baggy red sweatshirt; Liza wore jeans, a jeans jacket, and her nose ring; Patty wore brown pants and a red and white striped shirt; Don wore a red T-shirt and blue shorts, both stained with sweat, to go with his white basketball sneakers; Rudolph wore white pants covered in ketchup and a blue shirt; Honnie wore clothes the same as her friend, Liza.

Suddenly all of them were driven to their knees and they were all screaming. Black lightning flew between them, and the light from Quotient was so bright there was almost no visual of anything. The grass of the park turned to sharp, inflexible plastic.

However, Jen noticed a pair of key fundamental differences in the psychic representations of her alters and friends. One was Cara. The alters were not fighters, other than Cara, who was the alter that held Jen's childhood anger. Cara was roughly twelve years-old, lanky and mean looking, with stringy blonde hair. Unlike the others, she wasn't wearing clothes. She was wearing some type of battle armor that made her look like a giant gray bullet.

The other was Prisoner. Of all of Jen's alters, Prisoner was the most determined psychologically. This had grievously impaired Jen before she integrated, for Prisoner's function was to repress from Jen's memory Uncle Bill's attack, when he had raped Jen and her roommate in their college dorm room at Stanford. Uncle Bill had molested Jen for years, and when given a terminal diagnosis from cancer, snapped and attacked them both. He died during the attack, and Jen's roommate later killed herself. Oscar was probably correct when he theorized this was why Jen had been so eager to take a job where she could hide away from the world underground in the middle of nowhere, although Oscar had never shared his private psychological theory with Jen.

Prior to integration, Prisoner kept herself without a mouth and held in an asylum in Jen's mind, the representation of hiding the secret. She lived in a straitjacket, unable to move or speak; therefore, unable to give away the secret.

But now, she was standing next to Jen. Still in the straitjacket, she had a mouth, and her black hair was in a beehive formation, not stringy and messy like Cara's hair.

Cara was to Jen's left.

Prisoner shouted at the two of them, "I can grant asylum."

Jen had no idea what this meant, but suddenly the scene shifted. Jen nodded, then suddenly they were in the asylum where Prisoner lived, hiding her shame and the pain. The asylum wasn't pleasant, for it was merely a psychic representation of imprisonment and torment. Jen had been here when Oscar had helped her integrate her alters, and much more recently when they found part of her mind was being controlled as part of the plot to imprison and execute Meredith.

The walls were irregular and made of crumbling brick. Metal poles that were rusted held up the roof. The floors were broken, cheap linoleum in a pattern of black and white bars. Spiders the size of rats ran rampant on the floors and rats the size of cats lurked in the corners. The place smelled of rotten meat, and there were no attendants. Each corridor held cells with a small, barred window. Screams of despair echoed through the cavern, but above that was the sound of a wail like a hurricane.

"I've locked Quotient out, but not for long," said Prisoner to her team, which consisted of Jen, Cara, and Oscar.

"Why are we here? Where are the others?" asked Oscar worriedly. Knowing Quotient had the ability to consume souls, he feared Jen's other alters and Anissa had been . . . consumed. Oscar and Jen were both aware that her alters were actual souls, actual people without physical bodies sent by God to help her through her trauma. That revelation had come a few years ago . . . it was a defining moment in her life.

"I need you. Anissa must guard the others. *She* wasn't supposed to be here," said Prisoner quickly, nodding at Patty, who was cowering and holding onto Jen's right leg and sucking her thumb. Patty's face was dirty, and she was unusually quiet . . . in many ways, Patty was Jen's *original* personality, stunted by the trauma of seeing June murdered as a child. Patty tended to whine often and see Jen as a mother . . . but now she was simply quiet.

"What's going on?" asked Jen in panic.

"He's inside our mind, trying to kill our souls," said Prisoner.

Cara clanked a giant metal arm on her metal chest. Her odd battle armor had an opaque faceplate, through which the others could see her grim determination. It reminded Jen of a robot from a bad 1950s or 1960s science-fiction movie.

"Give me one shot at him with the thermo-nuclear device in my exterior housing and he's finished!" shouted Cara like a samurai.

"No. He's not bad," said Patty surprisingly and quickly. "He's just mad , 'cause we're hurting his friends."

"What are you talking about? He's a Nazi doctor," said Clegg, shaking his head.

"In the park, I felt like I did when Uncle Bill . . . did that to me," said Jen, referring to the rape in her college dorm.

"You're seeing your worst fear," said Prisoner. "That's what makes me immune. After our integration, I've faced mine. So have all of you, so you can push past the screen and see Quotient for what he truly is. Because of my mental strength and our unique abilities, I believe I can lock him away here, trap him forever."

"What is he?" asked Jen, dismissing the image of Uncle Bill raping her in the dorm room . . . she had seen him, the leer on his face, the messy hair, the pimple on his forehead . . . the fear, the helplessness.

She pushed it away. That trauma was in the past and could no longer hurt her unless he allowed it to.

"An alien of tachyons, dust, and light consolidated around some type of physical inner core. He speaks like Insectia but not like that. Telepathy, but we don't understand it," said Prisoner.

"Where are the others?"

"Anissa has them in the park. I brought those who can help with combat," she said, and pointing at Patty, "uh, like I said, other than her. She hitched a ride."

"I wanted mommy."

"What's Quotient doing? Why destroy souls?" asked Jen again and clarifying her question.

"He feeds of aural energy. He's trying to destroy our soul to eat, as if we were Big Macs," said Prisoner grimly.

The asylum was starting to brighten, despite the lack of lighting.

Jen snapped her fingers. "We're giving him problems. It's like when Insectia telepathically attacked us all those years ago. She didn't realize I was a multiple, more than a multiple with Anissa and Oscar — my psychological make-up is utterly unique. She thought I was a collective consciousness, one mind linked to others. I'm not. The same is true of our souls. I'm not just a body and a soul; I'm a body with many souls. He can't simply digest us like other humans."

"I agree," said Oscar, rubbing his chin. "We're like spicy Mexican food . . . he can't figure out how to eat us."

"Yes. But he's going to figure it out fast, unless Geneva and her team wipes him out in the exterior world," said Jen worriedly.

"Then let's stop blabbering like old ladies playing Bingo and kill him!" shouted Cara with exasperation.

"It's not that easy, Cara. We need him," said Prisoner, looking at Clegg. "*He's* the only killer we have."

Clegg looked down with shame and humiliation. "Very well."

Jen recalled their discovery a month earlier, how Clegg during his captivity in the concentration camps of the Nazis had been forced to experiment on his fellow captives, Clegg's great hidden secret in his life.

Cara's wresting of that secret from him had shamed him, left him more passive than in the past. Jen had been *liberated* by her integration and processing her secret, Uncle Bill's sexual attack at Stanford. The *opposite* had been true of Clegg, who had denied his guilt for decades and was being crushed by it. But then, Jen had been a victim of crime. Oscar had committed a crime, although under duress. Jen did not hold him morally responsible. He was a captive in a prison camp. But Oscar didn't feel the same, and his regret was weakening his resolve.

"Oscar, our lives are in your hands," said Jen.

"Don't hurt my friend, mommy," said Patty in a sudden whisper.

"Friend?" asked Jen in surprise. "What do you mean?"

"He wants to play."

Jen looked at Oscar and Prisoner, but they both looked puzzled. So Jen asked Patty, "Have you played with him already?"

"Just a little . . . before Prisoner came here. I got scared and came to look for you."

Time had no baseline relevance in the psychic world. Their entire battle and process could translate to just seconds in the outside world. Jen's integration had taken over a year in external time, but felt like mere hours inside her head . . . although to Clegg, it seemed to last forever as he spent much of it wandering in the corridors of their long-term memories.

"What did you do?" asked Jen.

"We're wasting time," snapped Cara.

Jen ignored her and knelt into a crouch to meet Patty at eye level. Patty looked oddly shy. "You guys prepare. Patty, how did you play?"

"We just played," said Patty, clearly not willing to share her secret with what was essentially her mother.

Clegg turned to Prisoner. "If I'm to attack, I must use the weapons I know, but we need to learn about him to stop possible future attacks. He may not be unique."

"Very well."

"I need drugs and an operating room."

"Done."

Jen rubbed Patty's cheek. "I won't be mad. You can tell me."

Patty put on a pout and said, "We just played tic-tac-toe."

The asylum began to shake and turn very bright. Quotient was obviously approaching. Prisoner approached. "There's no more time."

Jen stood and said, "Then let's shift."

Abruptly, they were on a grassy plain in what was obviously a war zone. Bodies lay in various states of half-death all around them, all male, all miserable. Gunfire was heard in the distance.

In the middle stood Clegg with a needle the size of a bazooka and a somber frown. Prisoner was dressed like a nurse, wearing a large white frock and skirt with a red cross on it.

"We have to act fast. I'll lure him here," said Prisoner.

Jen looked at Oscar. "What do I do?"

"I hope nothing. Help hold him while I 'drug' him."

Suddenly, Quotient appeared about ten feet in the air above Prisoner, who instantly collapsed on his return, unconscious. Quotient was so bright it was worse than looking into the sun on a July day. But Clegg ignored it and fired.

Quotient screamed.

Then Jen screamed as she felt a burning in her mind, a burning that made her want to rip out her eyeballs and turn herself inside out and tear her body apart rather than endure it any longer . . .

"Mommy, wake up!" shouted Patty, desperately shaking Jen's shoulders.

Jen woke up, on her back, hearing the sound of waves. She grabbed Patty in panic. "Quotient! Where is he?"

"I don't know. We were playing again, and he left me here."

"Playing?" asked Jen as she quickly scrambled to her feet. She was on a sandy beach that led to a bay of pink water under a hazy blue sky; it was hard to see where the fluid ended and the sky began. Two giant moons floated in the sky. To the other side was a rocky cave formation.

"Talking. And playing games."

"What did he say?"

Patty shrugged. "He's a little weird."

"How do you play with him? He's a ball of tachyonic light."

"He has a body, sort of."

"What do you mean? How do you know? Have you seen it?"

Patty shrugged and just said, "I just know, mommy. Uh, mommy, there's a woman over there."

Jen turned and looked more closely at an opaque golden orb sitting at the edge of the bay. Initially, she had thought it an odd rock, but now she could see Patty was right. Moving closer, she saw a woman with long, brown hair and a dowdy look trapped inside the orb.

This was Mary Richardson, although Jen did not know this, did not know Mary. Nor did she know Mary had been attacked by Quotient in San Diego on January 5 and had been an aural-lock coma since that date. Her body was cared for in the Las Vegas Special Operations headquarters. And, of course, Jen did not know Mary was a telepath.

Mary was banging on the inside of the orb, clearly shouting, but Jen could hear nothing.

"Mommy, we have to get her out. She can't swim."

"Okay," said Jen, touching the orb. It felt hot and pulsed, as if alive. Jen retracted her hand and said, "It feels like hot cauliflower."

"Yuck!" said Patty, taking a step back.

"She must be important. Is she another alter?" asked Jen of Patty.

"I don't think so. I don't know her."

Jen studied Mary's lips, trying to read her words. "I get some of this . . . Quotient . . . mental lock . . . coma."

Suddenly, Jen felt a tug on her shirt tails. She looked at Patty, who was pointing at one of the two moons.

It now had Quotient's face and was moving closer.

Mary turned to look as well and screamed.

Patty stepped forward. "Stop picking on my mommy! You're not nice! *We're not friends anymore!*"

"Friends?" asked Jen.

But there was no answer, for Quotient began to vibrate as if shaking himself or itself or whatever self to pieces.

Then thousands of tiny Quotients separated from the main body and flew at Patty, Jen, and Mary like squid.

They screamed. Jen grabbed Patty and covered her, knowing this was the end, that they were about to die and lose their souls.

The last image in her mind was the huge eye of Quotient starting down at them.

"*What the fuck?*" said Englehart.

He and Calico had been staring at the yellow, fog-like cone around the battle on the driveway.

And now they were suddenly staring at each other in the yard of the Kelkirk's home in Germany.

Calico looked alarmed . . . and confused. "We're . . . we're home?"

They looked up to see Quotient above them, vibrating.

"He did it," said Karla.

They turned to see her getting to her feet, having fallen to her knees on arrival. She said, "I don't know what happened in the battle, but he couldn't absorb their souls. I think . . . I think he got . . . *afraid*. So he brought us home."

Looking around, Calico said in a panic, "Yellow and Smith?"

"We're here."

They stumbled from a bush, Yellow pulling branches out of her blonde hair. She muttered, "What happened?"

Calico said, "That's . . . something we have to find out." Then she looked at Karla. "Did . . . he bring back Nile's body?"

"No."

"Damn," said Calico. "Then . . . today we grieve. Then we figure out how to succeed tomorrow. This delays us, losing Nile hurts personally . . . but this does nothing to stop the overall plan, simply makes it more complicated — while they sustained *heavy* losses today. Let them think on that a time."

Chapter Ten
Aftermath

"Geneva, wake up!"

The cold water on her face snapped Geneva awake. She was on her back, and she instinctively reached out to channel, but through a hazy and foggy view of a man, she stopped.

"C-Colin?"

"Praise the Lord for one favor," he said grimly. His curly hair was sopping wet and flat, and his cheek was scratched.

Slowly, she rolled to her right, propping herself up on her elbows, them behind her, giving her the shape of a reclining chair. Her head was throbbing, and the sun seemed very bright despite the fact that it was hidden behind a hazy fog.

"What . . . what happened?" she asked. Then she added, "You look terrible."

He did, covered in mud and sand, his clothes ripped and soaking wet, and plant debris stuck in his curly, wet hair. "I was slammed into the hillside. Jennifer is wounded. At some point, Quotient vanished and took Calico's team with her."

Instantly, Geneva was alert. Colin helped her to her feet. She was also covered in sand and soaking wet. She brushed sand away from her eyes and instantly started to remember the horrific final moments of their battle.

She stopped him. "Hold on . . . for a second. Colin . . . I almost lost my soul. I was so close . . . so close."

Colin nodded. "But you didn't, and I think the others need us. I'm the only one conscious so far."

Geneva nodded. "I understand."

Quickly, they found Jen. She lay on her back with her arms folded over her chest, as if posing for a coffin. Geneva gasped. "Oh, Jen. Oh, I failed you so badly."

"I tried to rouse her."

Geneva knelt next to Jen and rubbed her shoulder. Jen was also covered in sand and soaking wet. Then Geneva checked Jen's eyes. She did some additional basic response testing. But what struck Geneva was the reading she received when she read Jen's aura. Colin was looking down at them, arms folded over his chest, frowning, and asked, "Verdict?"

Looking up at him with a worried frown, Geneva said, "Her aura is . . . locked. This is what Tripper and I came across a few years ago with Golden Bear, when we found Heidi Minor.[4] It's not a physical coma. Her body is awake, but her soul is locked. We can't do anything for her except get her to Ops."

"I've only been keenly alert for five minutes. I tried to enter the rubble of the mansion, but it's impenetrable. The judges ran that direction for cover, and I'm worried Thunder and Ashley are inside as well. But I need help to dig the earth away, lost my totem when I was driven up the hillside. I searched around a bit to make sure those vile Consortium monsters were truly gone, and they are. The house has no power, and I've found no power source on the island. I don't know what we'll do when it gets dark, although we've a few hours before then."

Geneva nodded. "What about Crystal?"

Colin put a hand on her shoulder. "I'm sorry, m'dear, but she was struck down by Yellow. She's dead."

Shutting her eyes, Geneva said a prayer for her friend. Then she said grimly, "I'm sure this battle registered on Ops' readings. The instant they realize this is Mort's old island, they'll be here in force

---

[4] See TM 1.14 "Jennifer Saunders Saves the World – Twice"

and in a hurry, but even so, it's going to take a few hours. Let's survey the damages."

"Should we move Jen?"

"She's safe here on the driveway . . . at least, as safe as any of us."

Colin forced a smile. "We will overcome this."

Geneva looked at him and started to cry.

Colin held her. "Was it that bad?"

Geneva cried for a time before she finally broke the embrace and answered him. "The terror I felt . . . I was scared in Hell, Colin, but I had *hope*. When you start to lose your soul . . . there's *nothing* left of you. There's no hope."

"I'm sorry . . . uh, not to alarm you, but why did they leave, and what if they come back?"

"I assume we disrupted their plans and with Nile dead they can't carry them out, or we can hope that Jen somehow hurt Quotient, made him run scared," said Geneva. "And remember, they don't know who all we brought. They might think a second wave of agents is here waiting . . . has Radar shown up?"

"No."

"Odd."

Colin shrugged. "We can deal with that later. Let's check our friends."

They knew Meredith was dead. Geneva had the skill to cautiously and skillfully channel earth to move the debris without causing a collapse, despite her exhaustion from the combat with Quotient. They found Crystal's body, and she was obviously dead as well, her spine snapped by the falling pole.

Geneva said to Colin, "God, what a horrible day."

"Other than the fact that we did, at least, stop their scheme, I can't think of any worse," said Colin grimly. "I heard Crystal scream, but I couldn't turn. I don't know if her death was intentional or the pole just dislodged during the attempt to find safety in the mansion."

"I doubt anyone could TK a utility pole," said Geneva, unaware of Yellow's massive power. "Wait. Where are the judges?"

"I haven't seen them," said Colin grimly, and pointing at the massive pile of earth, he added, "I . . . assumed they went under. That's where they were running when last I saw them."

Geneva nodded. "If they were hiding, once Calico left, certainly 1040A would have come out to help. Damn."

"Let's try to dig out Thunder and Ashley and see if they made it. If they're in there, they could be hurt," said Colin.

Geneva nodded. "I don't think I'm ready to move that much earth yet, or stop some type of landslide."

"I think we have to start."

"Agreed there. Besides finding them, maybe we can find a generator or radio or phone or something."

They approached the mansion cautiously. Colin shook his head. Geneva put her hands on her hips and bit her lip as she studied it.

Finally, she said, "It looks like a Kansas twister went through. Half the place is fine, the other half rubble. If they're alive, they're . . . do you hear something?"

Colin was silent. Then he said, "Besides the obvious, tapping, over here."

They raced to the rear of the structure. Trees that had been growing in several feet of water behind the home were now gone. The tapping was louder.

"I think I can channel away the water," said Geneva, growing stronger by the minute.

She did so, and they found a metal hatch in a cement patio that previously had been hidden by the water. They opened it.

"Crickey, we thought we were goners!" said Thunder as he pushed Ashley towards the exit.

Ashley was a mess, having many severe cuts and bruises. Thunder looked shaken but otherwise okay.

"How did you get down here?" asked Colin, helping them out.

"I can channel electricity, got a sense for it. We were slammed into the house by that cyclone, which knocked out power . . . assuming this place ever had power. Anyhow, I sensed the generator, found the shelter, and we checked it out thinking Yellow and Smith might have hidden there. While we were in it, the rubble shifted and buried us."

"Some of these cuts are very deep and still bleeding," said Geneva, ripping up her shirt to use as bandages for Ashley. Geneva wore a sports bra underneath, so she didn't have to worry about her modesty. Nor would she have given the conditions.

"What's status?" Thunder asked, then he coughed up some dirt.

The four of them began moving towards Crystal's body. Colin said, "Our foes vanished, obviously portaled out by the alien. Other than the Neferates woman, they all survived intact to my knowledge. On our side, Crystal and Meredith are dead and the judges are missing."

"Blodgers are probably hiding in a coconut tree," muttered Thunder.

"Ops should have registered the tachyon disruption here. They should have someone here very soon, because this island is known to them," explained Geneva. "They won't mess around if there's an indication of activity here."

"I guess there's not much else we can — ouch!" said Ashley, wincing as Geneva accidentally scraped one of Ashley's deeper cuts on her left shoulder with a jagged fingernail.

"Sorry!" said Geneva wincing.

"It's okay. Uh, anyhow, there's not much we can do. The slide destroyed the generator, so there's no power here and none of us have phones. Quotient seems to have sucked all the energy from the island."

"Oh, God. Get away!" shrieked Geneva suddenly, running away from Ashley and towards Meredith's corpse.

The team looked up to see crows flying down to pick at the innards from Meredith's body. Geneva generated a wind and blew them away. "Bastards!"

Colin said to Thunder, "Let Geneva help Ashley and look for the judges. We should secure the bodies."

"Should we? Isn't this a crime scene?"

Colin shook his head. "This event today was a declaration of war. We know what happened here. Forensics are not important.

Furthermore, should the craven birds of prey fly away with all the bits, what evidence is there?"

Thunder shrugged. "Right point ya have there, mate."

"Besides, we have to find the judges. Logically, the only place they can be is in the ruins of the house. They could be alive."

Geneva was kneeling next to Meredith's body, the insides of her corpse strewn across the beach, having removed the metal poles from her corpse.

Gently, Colin pulled her away. "I'm sorry."

Geneva looked up at him. "Thanks. But she was as much your friend as mine."

"Very true. I will not see her murder go unpunished," he said with suddenly fury.

Geneva said sadly, "Calico . . . they probably felt they were defending themselves form an ambush. Still, her actions were too precise to be an accident. She wanted Meredith dead. But she's not her father."

"What do you mean?"

"She's not a random killer like he was. Kelkirk would kill someone who delivered the newspaper to the neighbor instead of him. Maybe he's mellowed with age, but not much. Calico was probably never that woman. She will kill for her cause, but only for the cause, to serve it or protect it. She would prefer not to, hence the Mars prison. She didn't kill anyone else."

Thunder and Ashley joined them, Ashley looking very depressed and in pain. Thunder asked, "What's that mean for us?"

Geneva shook her head. "I think we have to deal with her at that level, or we misunderstand her and therefore her motives. Miss that and we can't predict her actions."

"I don't feel so good," said Ashley.

"Let's get you out of the sun. I'll see what's in the flooded area of the house, maybe a room we can sit, or maybe some food."

"Geneva, let's secure our friends' bodies," said Colin gently.

Geneva knelt by Meredith's corpse and said, "May God bless your soul, Meredith, and give you the peace you never had here. I wish I had been a better friend."

Then she cried.

After a time, she went to Nile's body. "I regret you died, Nile. I pray for your soul and that God forgive and understand your crimes."

"You're a more forgiving person than I," said Colin.

"I was in Hell. Trust me, that changes your perspective."

Colin didn't know what to say to that, so they went to Crystal. "May God bless your soul."

"How you say, you give good prayer."

In shock, Geneva was on her feet and her eyes wide. She shoved Colin aside and laughed. Then she ran forward and hugged the gangly man suddenly appearing in the sand near them, much to Colin's shock and, frankly, chagrin.

"Who is this old fogey?"

"He's *Golden Bear*," said Geneva as if that explained everything.

Golden Bear was a century old, but he looked about sixty thanks to a combination of healing spells and glamours, which were how a TM was able to alter his or her base appearance and look older or younger. He was tall and gaunt, but emanated power. He had more wrinkles than a mountain range, and multiple age spots on his skin, which he didn't clean up with the glamour. His eyes were icy blue, almost white, and his teeth were dentures. Despite a prominent nose, he was probably attractive in his youth. His hair had mostly vanished, but there was a small, long ring left around the edge of his skull, all white. Geneva figured he was about six feet and eight inches tall. His arms and legs were skinny. Wearing old brown slacks, a yellow and black checkered shirt, and boots, he looked like someone having just stepped out of a retirement home.

In 2016, after years of searching, Geneva and Golden Bear's old friend, Tripper O'Sullivan, found him hiding out in Siberia working for the alien Lexx, who was running the Consortium. After having his operation dismantled, Golden Bear had returned to Atlantia with Queen Marrina, Lexx, and others. There, they had been working at helping Lexx return to his home planet, among other things. They achieved that in 2017, but it cost Marrina her life.

After that, Golden Bear returned to Russia, where he took residence in Moscow and began training Russian paranormals. He currently had a team of five.

"Rather cheeky name," muttered Colin.

"Golden Bear, it is so good to see you! Oh, thank God!" said Geneva.

"No, thank spatial gem. Well, thank God, too, and Yuri."

"Yuri? Who is he?" asked Geneva.

"He my secretary now. When tachyon surge register, he ignore all my warnings and interrupt me in the middle of meeting with Kremlin. Little Jack have me check out." He pointed up the cliff. "I arrive there a minute ago, asses."

Responsibility overwhelmed Geneva's personal needs to let her friends and family know they were safe. "You've got to get us back fast. Jen and Ashley need medical attention, and we had a devastating battle here against Calico Kelkirk and an alien, Quotient, one that not only murders mass numbers but destroys souls."

"That grim," said Golden Bear. Despite his Russian upbringing, he knew the soul existed. "I can stay here, so you talk to, how you say, Big Man at top. Little Jack."

"Colin, can you stay with him? He might need help, and I'd rather not explain to Ops just now who you are and where you're from."

"Of course, whatever you need, Miss Kane," said Colin with a smile, hiding his sorrow. He wanted to be with her, to help . . . and didn't want to be stuck with Meredith's corpse, stuck remembering how he had failed her in every way imaginable.

Geneva had another motive. She didn't know if there was a Little Jack in the parallel world or not, and if there were, she didn't want to have to explain to Colin everything that had happened here since 2018. It was best to just let this issue lie until the emergencies were dealt with.

"I have agent Sin Sam in Japan. He already on way. He be here before dusk with fancy stuff like generator and phone. We be fine," said Golden Bear, handing over the spatial gem to Geneva.

Portal and spatial gems enabled the holder to teleport across dimensions (portal gems) or localized space (spatial gems). The latter were rare and not known to exist until recent years. Golden Bear had one, given to him by Marrina some time ago. The tiny green gem was in a ring on his right hand.

Thunder and Ashley approached, Ashley leaning on Thunder for support. Thunder said, "Who's this old fart?"

"Later. Get ready to leave," said Geneva.

"Leave? How? You holding a lorry in that fist?" asked Thunder.

Geneva smiled.

Then they were gone.

The wind picked up, blowing Colin's wet hair. He assessed Golden Bear.

"You're a powerful man, Golden Bear. I can sense that even without paranormal skills."

"Da."

They moved to Meredith's body, chasing away birds again. Her guts were strewn across the sand, and they would never recover all parts of her. Colin reached down and rubbed her cheek. Thankfully, her eyes were closed at the time of death.

"I failed her completely, old man. In our world, I fought against Zenith for years. I met many allies, lost many friends . . . I started in this business when my sister, Nicola, was killed by a TM. But I have never failed someone as much as I failed this poor waif."

"Waif?"

"Girl. I failed her in court . . . she came to our world a stranger and was sentenced for crimes that . . . I couldn't prove weren't crimes. I failed her in battle. I should have been aware of her impulsiveness . . . should have been more keenly aware of the dangers."

Golden Bear patted Colin on the shoulder and handed him a flask of vodka he carried in his pocket. "Drink this. It, how you say, take sting off."

Colin took the flask, but didn't drink. He looked at her. "We'll have to find a container in the mansion or build something."

"I can take care of that, how you say, lickety-split."

Colin shook his head. "Meredith was the most tortured woman I've ever known. Maybe she's at peace at last."

"Drink vodka. It not really help with that, but it help forget."

Colin looked up, winked, and drank it in one swallow. Then he took Golden Bear's hand and got to his feet.

"You man worthy of Russian soldier," said Golden Bear.

Colin smiled. "I worked with many Russians in the parallel world. I can hold my own." Then he shook his head and looked at the sky. "I have a terrible feeling our failure here, however, means there may not be many days of vodka drinking ahead for any of us."

"Da."

"I doubt our esteemed judicial allies have made it," said Colin grimly, drinking a swig of vodka.

Then they heard something, a rustling in the bushes. Then a male voice said, "Hey, they made it!"

Colin and Golden Bear turned in surprise. "You must be Judge 1040A! EZ! Zounds!" shouted Colin.

The judges both came wandering from the hillside behind the house. Their robes had been destroyed, so they were running around in their underwear. Judge 1040A wore white briefs, while EZ wore boxers with pictures of hearts on them.

Coin raced to help them to the driveway, then shook their hands. "By the great one in the sky himself, you've survived! I'd given up hope!"

EZ pointed backwards and said, "Aw, we just took off runnin' and went up over that hill. Then there was a downhill slide and sort of a beach. This place isn't that big. I've been in bigger outhouses!"

Judge 1040A said, "I take it you're the good guys, since you haven't tried to kill us."

"Indeed. I am the esteemed Colin Ridgeway, and this is Golden Bear, hero of Russia."

"Da."

They shook hands, but Judge 1040A glared at Golden Bear. "Russia? Are you a commie?"

"Is that problem?"

"We're all friends here," said Colin quickly.

Judge 1040EZ said, "Geneva used to talk about a Colin. She liked him. Are you that guy?"

"Sort of. I'm the Colin Ridgeway of a parallel dimension, and when Geneva escaped back here, I came along for the ride."

EZ just looked at him, then said, "I need some better pot. I've never dreamed up anything like this."

"What happened here?" asked 1040A, looking around nervously, not all that confident in his rescue team. "Where's Geneva?"

Colin said grimly, "The rest of the team just portaled back to Vegas. We're going back after clean-up. As to what happened here, the answer is the simple, grim word — death. The gauntlet of war has been unleashed."

"War and I don't get along," said EZ quickly. "Uh, is there maybe some food in that house? Or clothes?"

"Who are we fighting?" asked 1040A.

"The Consortium killed Meredith and Crystal Jordan. We will bring them vengeance," said Colin.

"Crystal! Aw, no," said EZ. "She was always so nice to me."

"I know. Damn." Judge 1040A looked pissed. "This is a major bit of shit-ass news, British guy. What is this place?"

"One of their hideouts. Come, help us analyze the wreckage," said Colin, putting down the vodka, which 1040A immediately picked up and began finishing off. Colin added, "Then you can get back to civilization. The team is already working on counter-plans."

Chapter Eleven
Retreat

"What's wrong with him?" asked Calico of Karla, pointing at Quotient.

"I'm working on it. One moment. *^(^*&*."

Quotient responded with thoughts that both women heard. "()&(*&*(."

Calico's team was at her home in Germany, southwest of Dresden near the border of Switzerland outside a small hamlet called Dirkdorf, population 2,761. They had a large property outside of town and everyone left them alone.

The exterior had a paved road that was gated. The gate was red and white and locked. There was no guard post, and the chain-link fence around the four-acre property had barbed wire. The property had electronic surveillance. Behind the fence was a small airfield and two, yellow, metallic hangers. A blue and white tow-truck was usually parked next to the closest hanger, which was about a half mile away. The only other structure was a compact, two-story farmhouse with gray siding and white trim, surrounded by evergreens. It looked pretty but empty. There was a paved inlet from the road that led to the porch of the farmhouse.

The farmhouse was just a ruse. The real home was beneath the ground. There were four main levels, and below that was a huge experimental chamber, secured by concrete and titanium walls. The main chamber was a bordered by a control booth and several monitoring rooms full of servers.

Of the four main levels, the level just below the farmhouse was a guest-quarters, living quarters, and kitchen; essentially, it was a 2,000 square foot home laid out on one level, fully functional and able to be fully isolated from the rest of the complex. There were two elevators, on the north and south side, and two staircases, on the east and west sides. The staircases wound in circular fashion. The elevators were large, able to move an entire vehicle with load, several thousand kilograms.

The second level was for operations. This was mostly rooms for monitoring, either in large groups or in private, either locally or world-wide. There were six rooms in all. In the center was also a large conference room and a small kitchen connected to it.

The third level was research. The north half was labs. The south half was a library, consisting of books so rare Kelkirk had the only copies. Most were too fragile to scan, or even risk in pictures, though he had been working for years, off and on, to try and digitize the library.

The fourth floor was mostly maintenance and controls. It also had a workout room, locker room, and small gym.

And the sub-basement had the experimental chamber.

But for the moment, they were in the airplane hangar, which was large, open, and had sparrows nesting in the northeast corner. It was painted light blue and metallic. Inside was very little; a workbench with tools and several chairs and a table on which sat an old sandwich and a bottled water. There was a green and white, small plane parked nearby. It looked like it hadn't flown in some time, covered in dust and bird droppings.

Englehart entered from the outside. "Yellow and Smith were portaled back safely to the States. I checked and confirmed Quotient didn't bring back Nile's body."

Calico nodded. That was far down her list of concerns at the moment.

Englehart approached. Quotient watched him, the black protrusion that served as an 'eye' following the motions of Englehart's walk. It unnerved Englehart at times, times like this one when Quotient's state of mind was unpredictable. Englehart thought of him as a powerful dog that might turn on its master.

"What happened?" he asked Karla.

Karla turned to them. They were all still wearing the clothes from the island, having returned only ten minutes earlier. All were covered in sand and wet. Calico had taken the time to at least wipe her face clean of blood, though it was still mixed into her hair. She sighed and said, "All I can understand is that he was . . . playing."

"*Playing*?" said Calico incredulously.

Karla shrugged. "That's what I get, Calico. I don't understand it either. But he's also very weak now. He . . . he has to be fed, has to absorb some aura or he could turn on us. After all, that was the point of our spell on the island, to allow him to feed randomly throughout the world in a way that Ops wouldn't detect."

Calico nodded irritably. "I know. Damn. It would have fed him for months."

"We can't retry the spell," said Karla nervously. "There isn't time to set up, and besides, with Nile dead, we're one short."

Calico looked at Quotient, at once the most powerful and most helpless beings she had ever encountered. She folded her arms over her chest. It was infuriating at times. How could something so powerful be so difficult to understand?

"Well, we're weak, too," said Englehart, clearly put on edge by Karla's words. "Trying the spell again simply isn't an option."

"Then we'd better do something fast," said Karla anxiously.

"We have to go to *Mars*," said Englehart directly to Calico. "Ops will be all over us very soon. Kane knows about your father, and they'll figure out we're here."

"Don't underestimate my father. I'm sure Ops will *never* find us here," said Calico. "His tachyonic anti-matter field is also a quantum unified field. As soon as they find us, we appear to move."

"We're on Earth. They can find us. We killed two of their agents and held three hostage on Mars. Trust me, they will pull out all stops to bring us in," snapped Englehart, a rare moment of irritation.

"He's correct," said Karla.

"I'm not sure about that," said Calico, dropping her right arm to her side and holding her left. "But anything is possible."

But Englehart had another point. "We have to go to Mars and hide, and let Quotient have the auras of the fiftyish people still there to feed. If we let him feed here on Earth, that *certainly* will alert Ops. I'm certain your father, that no one, can put up barriers to block *that* type of tachyonic surge from Ops' detection."

Calico now looked angry and put her hands on her hips. Karla took a step back subconsciously, a clear action of keeping herself out of the middle of this discussion that had the potential to become a raging argument.

"The prisoners on Mars are just that, prisoners of this war," said Calico calmly but firmly. "The five people we were sacrificing were all aligned with Special Operations, a government organization, a military organization. Thunder and Ashley were actual members, and Crystal and those idiot judges helped them in the conspiracy. When one joins the military, or when one flaunts the rule of the land, one knows death is a consequence.

"But the other prisoners on Mars did nothing wrong except stumble into our plans in a way that risked exposure to us." She stared directly at Englehart. "Murdering war prisoners *is not* the way to start our new allegiance, to show the world the Consortium is the answer."

"This is a time for the practical, not the theoretical," said Englehart. "Calico, this *will* be a war, whether you want it to be or not."

"He's right," said Karla gently.

Calico looked at the ground. She nodded slowly.

Englehart pressed. "You know if we let Quotient feed here, Ops will find us. Storm Island had unique environmental conditions that shielded us. Those conditions don't exist in other places — that's why we picked it in the first place, though obviously it was convenient that Nile already owned it. And if we let Quotient feed, Ops will attack, and all our plans will have to go forward prematurely."

"We knew that was a risk."

"Yes, but we have a much, much better chance of success once Quotient is fully prepared and the situation Shy Strong has created is locked in."

Englehart knew he was right, and he knew Calico realized this intellectually, but was struggling with the emotional choice. Karla realized this as well and joined Englehart by adding, "Again, I agree, Calico. We're talking much greater odds."

Calico now faced the crisis moment every leader of every organization faced at some point or another. How she reacted would determine how the fate of the organization fared. Could she make the tough decisions? Could she make the right decisions? Were her allies trusted or merely yes-men?

And like every great leader, Calico finally simply had to make a decision. Refusing to decide was, in fact, a decision.

Slowly, she nodded. "This is true. We must move to Mars, make sure we're safe in case Ops does find this location and let Quotient feed."

Englehart put an arm on her shoulder, as did Karla. Englehart said, "I'm proud of you."

"I simply love you," said Karla.

Calico smiled. "I appreciate your support. This is hard for me . . . father ran things for so long."

"When do we go?" asked Englehart.

"How weak is Quotient?" Calico asked Karla.

"Weak, but he can manage a few hours, maybe even a day or two."

"We don't have to wait that long anyhow," said Calico. "Ops will come after us full force. Let's plan on eight hours. That gives us time to get all of the plans together and get the information out to our auxiliary agents, especially those in Strong's camp. Our shielding here should hold for that long, and I'd expect it to take several hours just for Ops to get to the island, let alone try to track us here in Germany." She paused and added, "We can monitor their progress from Mars. If Quotient feeds and is well, and there's no sign of Ops finding this place, we can return in a few days."

Englehart nodded. "Agreed. I'll take charge of all of the business. You secure your father's things, and Karla, you stay and tend to Quotient."

"Of course," said Karla.

"Thanks," said Calico to Englehart.

"It's my pleasure. What of Yellow and Smith?"

Calico frowned. "They have to stay on Earth. We need them to set up everything for the return, for the consummation."

"Ops wouldn't know them anyhow," said Englehart, and he was right. But because they had brought back *Colin* from the other dimension, Ops knew Yellow and Smith in *general* terms, something Englehart did not know.

"They'll know their appearance," said Calico. "But I guess unless they run into the grocery store at the same time, that won't matter much."

Englehart frowned. "An aural detector could pick them up, and they could have an aural lock on them. I don't know Geneva's skill."

Calico gave a mini-shrug and said, "Ah, true, but remember that aural detectors need relatively close range. The key, I think, is they can't be traced from the island. The aural trail ends where we portaled. It's as if we vanished."

"True enough. I don't think they are at any more risk than they were before all of this happened."

"I agree. Yes, maybe Geneva learned something they could find useful later. But I feel we have to take that chance. They're too entrenched, especially if we want to stay with the objective of implementation after the election and setting up a true habitat on Mars with indigenous animal life. Furthermore, we do have our man who is somewhat inside Ops' organization. We should get a tip if they're getting close."

"True. Well, we have backups for Yellow and Smith as well, but I would personally hate to lose them. They're special people."

"I agree," said Calico.

Englehart nodded and said, "Maybe we should leave it up to *them*. I'll contact them."

"Can we do it now? I'd like to know right away."

"Of course."

They exited the main hangar via a large door and entered an office that looked like the office of a lumber yard. It had a small desk, a lot of nails and screws on a table beside it, and a big artificial window on which was painted a green mountain.

On the battered and scratched maple wood desk was a laptop. Englehart contacted Yellow, normal procedure. He linked into the hangar's sound system so Karla could here while she worked with Quotient, making sure he stayed calm.

"Are you guys okay?"

"We're fine," said Englehart.

"That portal was a bit rough on Smith," said Yellow. "He's still throwing up. What's the plan?"

"We're going to take Quotient to Mars to feed on the prisoners there, keep him strong for the big moment," said Englehart. "Karla, Calico, and I will go as well. What do you two want to do?"

"We have to stay. We have a lot to do to prep things, unless you want the back-ups to move ahead?" asked Yellow.

"No, I want you," said Calico. "You deserve this, and your work is the best."

"Then we'll stay. But are you staying on Mars until the end?"

"No. We'll be gone perhaps a few days," said Calico.

"Very well. Can we set a date? I need to hear from you."

"One week."

"Good. God bless you all," said Yellow, and she blew them a kiss.

Eight hours later, life on Mars was proceeding, well, normally. Geneva's sarcastic description of it as a Residence Inn wasn't far off, but it was more like a few city blocks of completely self-contained living, like the Strip in Vegas or downtown areas of cold-weather cities like Minneapolis.

In the recreation hall, several people were playing board games.

"Bonus Yahtzee!" shouted Jenny McIver as she rolled dice against a former croquet player from India named Vishal Tendulkar.

"This game is rigged."

They were playing for chips, and Jenny pulled them to her side. On either side of her were two older women. The concierge of the city, Jenny was twenty-five, a petite blonde woman with very curly, short cut hair. She was very thin, and her brown eyes were wide. She was one of those people that was always up, always hyper.

Suddenly, her phone signaled an alert. She read the text and her jaw literally dropped. She said to Tendulkar, "Miss Kelkirk is here. I've gotta go!"

Leaving her chips and even her purse behind, she jumped into her golf cart, the most common form of transport, and raced for the gym, the most central room. She swiped her key card and entered the locked doors — this particular gym was used for events. There were other gyms for daily exercise. No events were scheduled today, so it was closed.

That schedule was about to change.

Once inside, Jenny gasped on seeing Calico in the flesh. Calico had the effect of a rock star on her.

"Oh . . . oh . . . oh, my goodness."

Calico put an arm on Jenny's shoulder. Calico had showered and changed into a gray suit and jacket with a yellow blouse and yellow booties. She looked coldly professional.

"Hello, Jenny. I need an assembly in one hour. Can you arrange it? We'll handle setting up the gym."

"Of . . . of course. What's going on?"

"Big news," said Calico with a thin smile.

Jenny's eyes brightened. "The *big* city is going to open?"

Calico winked. "I can't tell you that."

"I'm on it."

Jenny raced away in the cart.

Once she was gone, Calico turned and snapped her fingers. Englehart and Karla entered from other entrances. The gym looked like a high school gym, with bleachers and painted lines for basketball, although there were no hoops. The floor was dusty.

Karla wore a blue jacket and pleated skirt with white hose and shoes. Englehart even looked snazzy, wearing a black suit with a white shirt and white and yellow tie. He was tugging at the tie, obviously disliking it.

"How is Quotient?" Calico asked Karla worriedly.

"Weak, but he'll make it. Transporting us here took what little stores of energy he had left, but we've a couple hours."

"Stay with him. We'll work up here." Her reference was to the fact that the locker rooms were actually slightly below the main floor of the gym.

"Of course." She hurriedly exited.

Calico turned to Englehart and pointed. "Let's set up chairs, with a podium at the front, as if I'm giving a speech."

"Right."

They went to work silently. After half the chairs were up, Calico confessed, "This makes me sick, Englehart."

"I know. I feel the same."

"We're leading them to their death like sheep to a slaughter. This is not what I desired."

"I know."

Calico shook her head. "I don't know if I have the stomach for this."

"We have to. We knew there would be sacrifices, and we can't turn back now. Quotient must feed," he said, a mix between being pragmatic and delivering a gentle warning. After all, if Quotient were hungry enough, *they* could be on the menu.

During this talk, they had blissfully continued to set up folding plastic chairs. They were almost done now, with six rows of ten, leaving plenty of extra space right at center court.

"I guess we're ready," said Calico grimly. "This is going to be most difficult."

"I know."

She gave him a look. "Can't you say anything other than, 'I know'? Be useful!"

"Sorry. I'm nervous as well. But we're trading 54 lives for billions. That's what I keep reminding myself."

For a moment, she was silent. Then she looked at him, cocked her head, and said, "I know that . . . very well. I know if there were another way, my father would have found it long before he died, and I know the stakes. But . . . it's different seeing millions die in a city far away as opposed to leading helpless prisoners to their murders. Today . . . today I am simply a guard at a concentration camp, Englehart."

He had no words of comfort. He let the same. He hugged her.

She took a deep breath and put her hands on her hips. "But it must be done. Let's get it over with."

Jenny was thrilled. She had changed into a maroon blazer with matching skirt, black hose, red heels, and a white shirt. Behind the podium on the quickly assembled, elevated wooden stage that was only ten by ten feet in size, she said, "This is a great moment for Mars. I introduce you to the first and only President of Mars, Miss Calico Kelkirk!"

Everyone clapped. They had to. They feared the consequences if they didn't.

Calico came to the podium. She, Englehart, and Karla were standing to the right side of Jenny, the left of the audience. She simply said, "I am very sorry about this, but this is the first sacrifice to Mars we must make. I will pray for you."

Suddenly, Quotient appeared above the crowd.

They screamed and ran . . . no, they *tried* to run.

But they couldn't. Quotient had control of them. None of them could move.

Karla snapped, "*&)&)&&)&)!"

And Quotient fed on the souls of the fifty-four prisoners that comprised the population of the first city on Mars.

Chapter Twelve
Regroup

"Murder most foul," said Sylvester, shaking his head.

"To say the least," said Geneva.

They were in Little Jack's office, just minutes after Geneva's arrival with Jen, Ashley, and Thunder via Golden Bear's portal gem. Thunder had stayed with Ashley and was taken to an operating room, because one of the gashes on her leg was going to require significant work — by the end, she would have thirty-eight stitches and a large staple on the inside of her thigh.

Meanwhile, Jen was put in a medical room with Mary Richardson, still in the coma caused by Quotient's ambush in January. Given they were both rendered comatose during combat with Quotient, Sylvester wanted them together in case something happened — likely their recovery paths would be similar.

Geneva was still wet and covered in sand, her clothes ripped in a few places, her hair a mess. Little Jack looked anxious, beet red as he talked on the phone, trying to hurriedly set up a massive conference call with people scattered around the world.

To Sylvester, who was wearing a black pinstriped suit and a silver tie that made him look like a 1930s mobster, Geneva said, "Little Jack said he can have the team online within thirty minutes. We've got to get everyone involved. But while he does that, we have got to try and find any trace of the tachyon energy unleased on the island."

"Hold," said Sylvester. Then he removed his phone and held it up to Geneva as if to take a picture.

Stepping away in horror, she said, "This is no time for a photo, and you certainly aren't photographing me looking like *this*!"

"No. I'm running an aural detector app and overlaying it against a tachyon detector, like the one Sam Grant was using years ago when trying to track the portal Quafara wanted to open to resurrect Elkrod."

Geneva looked at him suspiciously. "That's okay then . . . I guess. I better not find pictures of me like this on the Internet." She was joking . . . mostly.

She held still. The phone made two odd beeps. Little Jack, meanwhile, hung up and said, "We'll be in the conference room five in five minutes."

"Good," said Geneva, watching Sylvester's expression change from one of analysis to one of worry. She had seen this look on men before: Jameson, Grant, even her husband Lon. "What's wrong?"

"You have residual tachyon particles in your aura. That's normal given the situation. But those particles have a *unique* signature. They're the same as those that were found in Mary after she was attacked and put in a coma, and now we also find them on Saunders."

"Mary was *what*?" asked Geneva.

"We need to talk before the meeting," said Sylvester.

"But can you find Quotient? If they're that distinct, you must be able to!" said Geneva with alarm. "We're talking about something that destroys souls, Sylvester! This is *urgent*!"

Sylvester shook his head. "Miss Kane, you miss the point. The app *doesn't* register these particles anywhere, other than in the sick bay on Mary and Jen. They must know how to disguise their trail when Quotient moves. They could be *anywhere*."

"*Damn*," hissed Geneva through clenched teeth.

Suddenly, a call came to Sylvester. "Oh, I see. That is good news. Will you two remain on the island? Ah. Ah . . . they can stay for a time, most certainly. A naval ship should be there within the hour."

When he hung up, Geneva asked, "Who was that? Colin?"

"Yes. The judges have been found alive and unharmed, though their clothes were ruined."

She shook her head. "They're luckier than a pair of cats!"

"Indeed."

Then she shook her head. Finally, she said, "Okay, well, I'm glad they're good, but we have serious business. You said five minutes, right? So I need to call my mother and call Lon."

"Well, it's so good to hear from you, my daughter. I knew you were alive *somewhere*. When one's daughter escapes Hell, you just figure she's in another dimension somewhere. Where were you this time?" said Geraldine with humor. Of course, she felt much more ambivalent about her daughter disappearing without trace — again — but she had faith Geneva would return eventually.

Long ago, she had resolved that being the mother of a Special Ops agent had challenges of its own. Geraldine had been in the field herself until permanently injured by the TM Reddy Otero. She knew the risks of working in Ops. But she also knew of her daughter's dedication and big heart.

"Mars."

"Mars? Oh, how quaint. Better than Hell, I take it," said Geraldine.

Geneva laughed. Hearing her mother's voice was so soothing to her it was almost like taking a drug. "Well, that depends on your point of view. It was more like being trapped at a Residence Inn in Boca Raton."

Geraldine laughed. "I'm glad your back then! Your sister sort of felt you one day."

"I figured as much. Look, I need to call Lon, and we're going to meet here shortly."

Geraldine saw another line flashing and said, "That's probably the conference call now. I'll talk to you shortly. I love you."

With great emotion, Geneva said, "I love you, too, mom, more than you'll ever know."

Geraldine hung up with tears in her eyes. So did Geneva. But then she smiled, dialing her husband.

Lon was wearing a gray suit and was energetically directing some construction workers assembling a scaffold at a rally in Cleveland for a President Trump press conference scheduled for the next day. Standing in tall grass and bright, unusually hot late afternoon sun, he smiled and said, "You don't write, you don't call, what's a husband to think?"

"You didn't send me roses," she countered.

"I didn't know where to send them."

"Mars."

Lon was silent a moment. "Huh?"

"We're going to conference in with Ops shortly, but I was kidnapped by Kelkirk's people in Antarctica, sent to a prison on Mars, and then I escaped into the parallel dimension and Jen Saunders and friends helped me get back. We then battled an alien named Quotient that eats souls and lost."

There was silence for a moment. "And I thought working in Cleveland was strange. Are you joking?"

"Nope. It's deadly serious. Millions are at risk, husband."

"Damn. And I thought I was engaged in risky work protecting Trump at these rallies." He sensed the grave tone of her voice and knew her spirits needed bolstering with humor.

She laughed. "Given his poll numbers, you might be at real risk." She paused. "There's one other thing. After this meeting, I have to come home and assemble a team and rest for a few days. On my way home, we're going to meet somewhere and I'm going to make love to you until we're too sore to do it ever again."

"That is a date! My God, I love you."

"I love you, too. How is your life?"

"Well, Tripper assured us you were alive, but it's hard. I've missed you so much. Your mom and sister have kept me going. Your sister has become quite the little family leader in your absence."

"Really?" said Geneva with genuine astonishment.

"Really. She's growing up at last."

"Maybe," said Geneva skeptically. "Well, I'm glad you knew I was okay."

"I knew but I didn't know. I don't have the faith of your mother. I'm damn glad to hear your voice at last."

'Me, too, baby, me too. We'll talk again soon. I love you."

"I love you, too, more than anything in the world."

"I, too, more than anything in this world . . . or Mars."

Geneva then quickly cleaned up as best she could. She still looked like she had been dragged through the swamps of Louisiana after Hurricane Saturday. Her hair was a mess and soaking wet, but at least she could shower and get the mud, sand, and twigs out of her hair and off her skin. Ops' staff brought her a change of clothes, nothing fancy, just jeans, black heels, and a white sweatshirt with a pink, collared undershirt.

She took about two minutes to quickly read the bios of everyone involved to see what she had missed the last few months. Geneva could read fast.

Then, focusing on the future, she exited the room and headed for the conference room and the start of the final war with the Consortium.

"I'd be flattered at the attention if the situation weren't so grave," said Geneva with a polite, businesslike smile as she entered Little Jack's main conference room, which he and Joy had refurbished. There was a portable rectangular table like those seen at bake sales on one side of the windowless room. On the other three walls were eighty-five-inch television screens, a total of twenty. There were six each on the two short walls of the rectangular room and eight on the longer wall, opposite the table.

At the table sat Little Jack, wearing his typical pinstriped shirt and baggy black pants. The only other person in the room was Joy Delaney, the paranormal who could control people and Little Jack's girlfriend. Now twenty-seven, while very pretty, she wasn't gorgeous. She had a nice figure with round bottom and breasts, good legs, and a happy face. Her hair tended to be straight and parted in the middle, and although a natural blonde she often dyed it lighter. Her eyes were a dull blue, her face pretty even with her nose being a little big. Joy was the type of girl that looked good in nice clothes and make-up, looked average without them, and basically was pretty enough that she could get by if she was willing to play to her assets. She wore a white, frilly, sleeveless vest over a blue blouse with white pants and a black double-belt. Her heels were red.

"How are you, Joy?" asked Geneva.

"Fine," she said, but she looked scared and worried. "You look good."

Geneva smiled. "It's nice of you to lie, but I look and feel like crap. Things are bad."

"C'mon, we'll help," said Joy, and she led Geneva to the table.

In Las Vegas, it was almost noon. The staff had left some chocolate chip cookies, bananas, and coffee. Joy had some coffee. Little Jack and Geneva declined, their gray coffee mugs left empty.

Geneva took a seat in the portable gray metal chair opposite Little Jack, she now being nearest the door. She took a big handful of cookies. Little Jack said, "I'll connect us all. You talk. Whoever you don't know, if anyone, we'll deal with later."

Geneva was astonished at the assemblage. She did know everyone present; after all, she had been an agent for fifteen years.

On the far screen of six were faces she knew: her mom, basically an older version of Geneva; Medina, her sister, a blonde and sassy, picturesque blonde; her dark-haired, handsome, white-toothed husband Lon; Tripper, wearing shades and his Atlanta Braves baseball cap and hiding behind a big black beard; Tripper's old flying buddy Rhino, who looked like a less handsome Gene Hackman; and redhead, blue-eyed pixie Searly McTaggert.

On the long wall were eight more faces: retired Ops director General Emerald Jon Jameson, with salt and pepper beard and mustache and emerald green eyes, the long-time director of Ops and the man in charge when Geneva had joined; General Oglesby, who looked like a 60-year old, fat, black defensive tackle; General Carrington, a thin face with droopy eyes and a thin black mustache;

Sylvester Starnes, the Immortal Man, who currently was the director of Ops and who was in the next building over in the trauma center because he wanted to finalize the security and setup of Jennifer in the hospital wing; Sly Silverman, a cute blonde with blue eyes and a friendly face who had just joined Ops earlier in the year; Lottie Russell, and older woman with long blonde hair who was the current Ops liaison with the Vegas police; and chubby-faced Mark Meachum and brunette Kylie Keller, those two representing the Neutrals, a group of non-conscious paranormals that unofficially worked with Ops from time to time.

On the near wall was Sam Grant, who had quit as director when Meredith 'died' in 2018 and 'retired,' although he'd engaged in several active field assignments; Kacie Siu, who Geneva had worked with in the Orient; and finally Golden Bear and Colin from Storm island, where they were still coordinating events.

Thunder and Ashley arrived internally. Ashley looked much better being clean, bandaged, and her right arm in a sling. She wore a yellow blouse, jeans jacket, jeans, and black shoes. Thunder had cleaned up and wore a white collared shirt and olive pants.

Geneva stood at the end of the table and said, "I am honored at your attention. Little Jack and I have spoken briefly before the meeting. I'll speak, and Jack stop me if I go wrong."

"Sure."

"I cannot impress on you the grave, urgent, and dire nature of what we face." She looked at Jameson, then Sam, then Tripper. "We've stopped Quafara and Elkrod. We stopped Lexx. We stopped all the crazies in 2017. And Tripper and I went to Hell. *None* of that compares to this. We face a team of known TMs, primarily the Consortium TMs, who seek to save Earth by establishing life on Mars, and to do that they are going to use an alien that powers tachyon particles by consuming auras . . . consuming *souls*. To achieve the goal, it must consume millions."

She paused. Everyone looked either shocked, grim, or angry. None of them doubted Geneva. Of everyone in Ops, at this point she was the most powerful, the most respected, and a person of the highest moral integrity.

Geneva added, "We were always suspicious of the Consortium's motives. We were right to be so. Now, we have to stop them."

Sam finally spoke. "For those of us in the field and not always able to access daily reports, just take us from A to B. I assume this started when you vanished?"

"Almost. On January 4, Sheila Warren was killed while on a simple research expedition in Antarctica. I went with a team that had trained under Golden Bear's new European-Russian consolidation of Ops. On arrival, we found Sheila's phone. She killed herself to avoid having her soul consumed by the alien, who we now know is Quotient."

"The same Quotient that Marrina stopped in 949," interjected Sam.

"Yes. We assume so. We assume the Consortium found him in the ice using agents on the inside at the Antarctic base and freed him. Anyhow, I was betrayed. The team I was with was part of the Consortium, and I was ambushed by Calico Kelkirk and two of her allies, Karla, and Englehart, and kidnapped."

"Explains while I no find them. They are, how you say?" said Golden Bear.

"Scum-sucking traitors?" suggested Little Jack.

"Double-agents."

"Yes," said Geneva. "Anyhow, the phone recordings made it clear via the Ops' aura app that the souls of those on the base were destroyed by Quotient. You can see it clearly. Other than Sheila, of course, bless her."

"God damn," said Tripper. Then he took a swig of moonshine from the flask in his cane.

"I was knocked out and awakened in Kelkirk's castle in Germany. Kelkirk outlined the Consortium's plan. They would move mankind to the Moon as global warming has passed the point of no return. To do this, Quotient would consume millions of souls. He also indicated something is going to happen later this year that will prove the necessity of this need."

"Something?" asked Sam.

Geneva nodded. "Yes. It was . . . as if to make a point. So either they know it's going to happen or *make* it happen. Anyhow, I then threw a quite justified but somewhat childish hissy-fit, so he left me to sulk," said Geneva sheepishly. "Anyhow, a short time later, Calico informed me that Kelkirk had died, apparently of natural causes."

"Really? I don't believe it," said Sam.

"I can't prove it one way or the other, but I'd wager my boot collection that Calico was sincere, Sam. She was grieving. Anyhow, she also informed me she was Kelkirk's *daughter*. I thus assume now *she* is the leader of the Quotient-Mars plan."

"The QMP. We'll need an acronym for this," said Jameson dryly, trying to lighten the mood.

Geneva nodded and didn't smile. "Fine, Jon. The QMP. Okay, anyhow, while I was there telling Calico I'd never agree to help them or let them get away with it, I was zapped to a prison." She turned to Jack. "From what I've learned, the next day Quotient appeared in San Diego and knocked Mary into a coma."

"Yep."

"And when Heidi Minor, the new Marrina, challenged the Gods, she was killed and the Gods fled."

"Yeah," said Little Jack, clearly still somewhat unnerved by the memory of Donovan handing her a jar of Heidi's ashes.

"Meanwhile, I soon discovered we were in a prison on Mars. That's where I met these two, Thunder and Ashley, missing since November. I also found the judges and Crystal Jordan."

"And we are all so glad you're back," added Joy with a smile.

Geneva continued. "They were portaled there as well, though not by Quotient, so presumably by a portal gem. Portal gems that we know of can't do this, so they must have found one that has capabilities unknown to us. Yet another problem." She took a deep breath. "For four months, I've been using the probability cloud influence in my channeling to try and get us home. Through a mind-boggling complex series of events I'll detail when I have time, I wound up in the parallel dimension. From there, Jen was able to get me back.

We arrived on the island where Searly and our dear, departed Clarke Kent fought Mort and Nile in 2010, Storm Island."

"That place! *Holy crap*! It hasn't sunk yet?" asked Searly in surprise.

"Not quite. Anyhow, Calico and her cronies were preparing some sort of ritual that would have sacrificed the paranormal prisoners from Mars, possibly to feed Quotient by destroying a few dozen souls, but more likely doing something to prep for Mars move. We stopped them." She winced. "It cost Crystal her life."

"Damn," said Jameson, speaking for all of them.

"Yes and . . . but now we can't find any trace of them." Geneva took a breath. "When we came back from the parallel dimension, we came back with some . . . some others. The most radical is Radar, who Sam, you will know as Meredith's uncle, John Patience."

"*Alive*?" asked Sam with obvious surprise.

"Son of a bitch," said Jameson with equal surprise.

"Yes. Zenith tried to kill him, as you and Meredith surmised many times, but while she failed, she did manage to trap him in the parallel dimension. We had a reading that he was dumped in the ocean a few hundred miles away from us on arrival — he's a robot, so we know he's safe."

"A *robot*?" asked Sam incredulously.

"We can talk more about that later," said Geneva. "It's more urgent to find Quotient. Radar has some precognitive abilities, he's a seer. He spoke of key events in the near future that could cataclysmically merge our worlds. Obviously, Calico and the Consortium are the source."

"Reckon that's easy to figure why y'all can't find 'em. Kelkirk's skanky daughter and an alien damn sure straight can hide like a cottonmouth in tall grass," said Tripper.

"They don't need to," said Jameson. "Obviously, they can get to Mars. Why hide here when they can hide there?"

"Sure," said Thunder, snapping his fingers. "Hell, even if we find them, we can't get there."

"The spatial gem!" said Geneva, pulling it out.

"Too far," said Golden Bear. "Spatial gems are, how you say, local travel only. Local being Earth."

"We have to stop them," said Geneva in despair, running her hands through her hair.

"Agreed," said Sam quickly.

Searly added, "Damn straight."

There was a pause.

"Do we?" asked Little Jack suddenly.

"What?" asked Geneva with utter shock.

"I mean, they want to save Earth. That's a good thing. Maybe we could get them to drop the Quotient thing and work with us to put man on Mars?"

Geneva stood up and walked to stand before him. He looked surprised. Then she took his coffee mug and slammed it into the table so hard the mug and the table cracked. In a cold whisper that sounded like shotgun blasts that made the hairs on Little Jack's neck raise, she spoke.

"We will not consider negotiating with soul-murderers as a viable option!

"Is

"That

"Understood?"

Little Jack for once didn't know what to say. Her face was inches from his, and he would have sworn she was a wolf waiting to eat him. He just nodded, drool escaping the corner of his mouth.

Geneva turned to the screens. "Any *other* dissension?"

There was dead silence until Sam, with a smile, finally said, "I think we're all on board, Geneva."

"I sure am," said Joy quickly.

"Good," said Geneva.

Little Jack cleared his throat and said, "I just . . . I'm the boss. I have to play every angle. I'm with you."

"Good." She sat back down. Then she said, "I guess we have two plans. First, we have to try and trace where they are at if they are on Earth. Second, we have to come up with a way to get to Mars.

Everyone has to be ready. This is more important than anything we are working on."

"Even finding Chase," agreed Searly, Chase's best friend still trying to find where Chase disappeared to after the February kidnapping. [5]

Geneva hurt as she said this, having read of Chase's disappearance on file, but it was true. She wished it wasn't. "Yes."

Jameson said, "Are we sure *Chase's* disappearance isn't part of the Consortium-Mars plan?"

Little Jack answered. "Yeah, we're pretty sure."

"Maybe the WSA can help with that," offered Jameson.

"They already are, Jon," said Sylvester.

Sam said, "Chase isn't connected that we know of, but at this point, it doesn't matter since we can't find her." Eager to change the subject from their failure, Sam said, "You're perfectly correct, Geneva, but thinking outside the box, there's one other area to look into. Well, actually two, if I may offer them?"

"Of course, Sam," she said, eager for his input.

"Well, first off, if Mary and Jen both survived against Quotient, why are they alive and why hasn't he come back to *finish* the job? I mean, I know Little Jack has us shielded — God knows how he got that through the budget — but they haven't even tried anything else, not any conventional means. Jen and Mary have very unique mental states — Mary is a telepath and Jen a 'soul' survivor. There may be something there we can use, something that is protecting them."

Tripper chimed in. "Reckon he's right."

Geneva said to Little Jack, "I'll trust you can form a plan to do that?"

"Of course."

"The other thing," said Sam, "is I'm starting to wonder now if this upsurge in totem movement we've seen since '17 is also part of the plan. You said Radar said something is going to happen, so I'd bet dollars to donuts those fuckheads in the Consortium are going to

---

[5] See TM 3.2 "Identity"

make it happen. Stop that and we might stop their plan, even if we can't stop Quotient."

"I concur," said Sylvester.

Little Jack said, "Going along with that . . . I have some feelers out into the Society of Jack-O'-lanterns. I have a suspicion they're tied in as well. Many of the key Consortium members are members of both."

"They've been flying under the radar since I was in charge," said Jameson.

Carrington quickly said, "It's worth researching. I've tried to look into them, but I always get blocked via the normal military channels. You might have better luck."

"I hope so," said Little Jack. "Anyhow, all of that will take time. Let's find them and study Mary and Jen immediately."

"Agreed," said Jameson.

"I appreciate all of your help," said Geneva emotionally. "I've been desperate to get back to my friends and family and save everyone. We will win. We must win!"

They clapped for her.

Then she wiped away a tear and said, "Ah, one final note: Sam, I need to talk to you privately about some personal information after our meeting. Can you and Searly stay on-line?"

"Sure, for a time," said Sam. Searly just nodded.

"It shouldn't take long."

"Good."

Sam Grant was attending via remote session while sitting in the sixth floor of a mostly empty office building overlooking a park in Tampa Bay where Shy Strong was holding a campaign rally. Florida was a crucial state in her hopes to win the 2020 Presidential election, and she was neck and neck with Trump in the state. Sam was wearing a red and white checkered shirt, jeans, and old white sneakers.

He was extremely surprised by Geneva's public request for a private meeting. All he knew was it had to be urgent. Once the room cleared, he felt very tense.

The room around him was empty. It had six cubicles and shelves, but no other furniture. It was also dark, on the side opposite the sun. Dark and quiet.

Geneva said, "Sam, we're alone except for Searly."

"Hi, Sam. How's Florida? Got any lemons for me? The ones here in Nebraska suck, though don't ever tell that to my in-laws," said Searly with a smile.

"I have a pain in the ass, but no lemons. Geneva, what did you need? You said personal, so I assume you need a friend and not a brilliant Ops tactician."

"Oh, spare us," said Searly with a giggle.

Geneva didn't smile, didn't laugh. "Sam . . . this is going to hurt a great deal."

Sam felt a knot in his stomach. "Hit me with it, Geneva."

"It's . . . about Meredith."

That was *not* the name expected. "Geneva, she's been dead for over two years. If you learned something about her that is going to hurt me, I'd just as soon not know it."

"It's not . . . not that at all." And then Geneva started to wipe away tears. "God, I . . . Sam, she . . . she survived Mount Saint Helens."

"What? *What*?" said Searly like a parrot. Her first 'what' was said in a whisper, in shock, the second a loud exclamation of surprise or denial.

Sam just stared. "Come again?"

Geneva breathed deeply and sucked up her tears. "When I was on Mars, Thunder and Alicia and Crystal and the judges helped me portal, using some sort of odd link to the probability cloud. There's some type of relationship between Quotient's tachyon surges and the PC, but we can get into that much later. Anyhow, I woke up in Jennifer's world."

"I read this in the synopsis you guys emailed just before the meeting."

"That was just the synopsis, Sam. I need time to finish the detailed report. Anyhow, when I got there . . . Meredith was there."

"In Jen's world? How? She was able to shift in space, not across dimensions."

"I don't know. I assume it was a mix of desperation and the odd channeling David Mize's subconscious was using on her at the time she was sacrificed to the volcano by Everett. At least, that was Joshua Clegg's theory, and I buy it."

"But . . . this . . . I see," he said, looking ashen.

Sam had loved Meredith as much as he had loved his wife, Bam, who was killed in combat against Shanna McGruder in 2014, impaled before Sam's eyes. But with Meredith, it had been a challenging, stormy relationship. Not their love; in that, they were always solid. But in trying to heal Meredith from the repeated trauma, the PTSD, and the rage, Sam had to deal with a constant, underlying tension.

In that, he never felt he succeeded. Most days, he felt like their relationship was her only solace in a troubled life that she hid behind a veneer of being cocky and sassy. He was the only rock on her shore.

When she was murdered on Mount Saint Helens, he never felt the despair he felt when Bam was died. He just felt . . . empty. That had lasted for months as he drove around the country, spending time with Jameson and other old friends.

To a degree, he had never put her death behind him. Hell, he had never put *Bam's* death behind him. He never would — she had been murdered right in front of him. But Meredith's death was different. He had loved Bam with all his heart and soul and in their relationship they were equals. And although he lost her, he knew she had lived a fulfilling, worthwhile life, that she had overcome the difficulties that led to her manslaughter charge, had turned her life around and was at her happiest in the final years of her life, her years with him.

With Meredith, he felt the opposite, that despite all he tried, she just kept sinking and sinking . . . that when she tortured and killed Necra, she essentially was torturing and killing herself, creating a situation she could never come back from. He couldn't stop it. He didn't particularly try, because he knew that had to come from within her . . . and it didn't.

Bam had a normal life. Sure, it had sadness; her parents had separated, she had shot Jamal-Williams, she had served nine months in prison, all tragic and depressing events. But not unique.

Meredith had *not* lived a normal life. Hers was one of repeated trauma. She came home from school at sixteen to find her parents murdered and her sister enslaved.

Which was probably the key to Meredith's entire life. She was a traumatized child and never escaped that.

"Sam. Are you okay?" asked Geneva.

Sam shook his head, pulling himself back to the moment. "I . . . I don't know. This is . . . I don't know how to feel. I mean, she's been dead for over two years, or at least to me . . . it wasn't like when you've vanished. She was on top of an exploding volcano. Even for a comic book fan like me, I couldn't envisage escaping that."

"I know."

"I . . . what happened?"

"In short, she somehow portaled across dimensions but was comatose in the parallel world with Saunders until just a couple of months ago." Geneva paused, deciding to leave out the stuff about the trial. It served no purpose now. "She was the main reason we got back, some weird channeling I did with Radar, also using Jen's alter selves and soul survivors. We could never replicate it in a million years."

"I . . . I see."

"The probability cloud aspects of my channeling took us straight to Quotient's team, and she killed Nile before Calico killed her. Meredith took the lead, Sam . . . she was a heroine. She was brave."

"Of course, she was. Lack of bravery was *never* her problem."

Sam was quiet. Geneva said, "How do you feel about this, Sam?"

"Just . . . shocked. Honestly, the past few months I've been so busy with this stuff surrounding totem movements that the Neutrals now think is tied to the Presidential campaign . . . I've been keeping busy to avoid thinking, but it's also important, helps. Uh . . . I don't know what to feel."

Geneva said, "Sam, I . . . you're not a former boss to me. You're my friend. If you need anything, emotional or otherwise, I'm here for you."

"Is . . . I mean, is there a salvageable body? Her casket is empty, as you know," he said, referring to Meredith's original funeral in 2018.

"There is."

"I'll take care of it. Let whoever needs to know put me in touch with whoever can ship it. I can't . . . I guess I can't rebury her in Lake Forest?"

"Perhaps you should."

"Yeah, fuck, if Ops can't handle it, Clint will help me out," he said, referring to his former boss at the National Security Association, where he had worked prior to joining Ops in 2005. Sam smiled. "I appreciate that, Geneva. You're a rock, always were. I never had to worry about Miss Kane, and I appreciate that. That hasn't changed now that you're Mrs. Kane either. You ever going to change your name?"

Geneva knew this was Sam's way of changing and thus closing the subject. She winked. "Why change a great name like Kane?"

"You got me there."

"We'll keep in touch, my friend."

"Of course. You need rest. You must be exhausted. See your family and husband."

"I plan to."

"Until later, Mrs. Kane."

"Until later, Mr. Grant."

"Sam, stay on a minute," said Searly.

Once Geneva signed off, Searly said, "I'm really, really sorry, Sam. What can I do to help?"

"It's okay, Searly. You need to find Chase. *We* need to find Chase. I don't know how much we can do towards saving the world from Quotient."

"Don't change the subject. I know you're upset," she said.

"Yes . . . I think I just need some time."

"Okay." She paused. "Call me tomorrow, okay?"

"I will. I promise. Thanks, Searly."

"You're my friend . . . my best friend. Okay?'

"Okay."

She signed off and Sam just sat for a time, thinking, remembering all the times he and Meredith had shared together. He felt like someone had sucked out his soul and spit on it.

"Good to see you two," said Little Jack after the meeting to Thunder and Ashley. "C'mon, let's talk in my office."

Thunder nodded. He and Ashley followed. Ashley said, "This stupid sling is fucking annoying."

Little Jack laughed. "We'll get you a custom one."

"How about one with a laser, like those science-fiction robots have, to blast Calico?"

"I'll work on it," he said.

The elevator opened and Little Jack used his fingerprint to open the door. They followed and took a seat in front of his desk.

Little Jack said, "You have no idea how glad we are that you're back. We've been searching since November. What happened?"

Thunder said, "We'll file a report, but basically when we were in Perth, we got ambushed by the late, great Nile Neferates and zapped to Mars, where we spent a few months being stuck on *The Prisoner*."

"That show with Patrick McGoohan? I loved that show!" said Little Jack, clapping his hands.

Thunder laughed. "It's more fun *watching* the show than being part of it!"

Ashley added, "You'd think being on another planet would be this life-changing experience, but it was like being stuck in a hotel by the airport with your flight perpetually delayed."

"Crickey, you got any Marlboro Lights, Jackie?"

"Little Jack, please, and we're a no-smoking building," he said.

"Right. Bloody hell. Sorry, Little Jack."

"Forget it," he said with a wide smile. "Do you two want to help or go home to your families?"

"Are they safe?" asked Ashley with alarm. "I mean, won't the Consortium go after them for revenge?"

Thunder said, "I don't think so."

"Neither do I or Geneva," said Little Jack. "Calico has gone out of her way to avoid killing anyone unless it was part of the Martian objective, like trying to sacrifice you. Or killing Jordan or Patience. Besides which, we really have no way to stop them. I've got a field around this place, but it cost like six figures a day to run. I can't put it around everyone."

"Of course," said Ashley. She looked sad but resolved. "I'd like to visit my parents in Centralia, let them know I'm okay."

Little Jack looked guilty, then said, "Well . . . okay. Let's get this out now. They don't know you're missing."

"Come again?"

"Guys, when you vanished, we didn't want your families to panic. So, we put it to them that you went deep undercover and would be gone months, maybe a year, to buy us time to find you. We fed them, ah, updates. So, well, they're not as upset as you might expect."

Ashley nodded. "Well, that's actually a relief. I love them. I've missed them. I'd hate for them to worry. But we have to stop Calico."

"Too right," said Thunder.

"Well, we have nothing urgent. Why don't you take a few days and see them, then check in? When we get a lead, we'll send you off," said Little Jack.

"I'd like that," said Ashley.

"I'll take care of it. You two like working together?"

Ashley looked at Thunder, shrugged, and said, "Ahhhhhhhhhh, I've worked with worse."

"Bloody insolent sheila." He laughed. "We make a right fine team, mate."

"Okay. Good to know. Oh, by the way, those two judges were found by Colin safe and unharmed."

Thunder slapped his forehead. Ashley said, "Great. The ultimate paranormal battle where people die and wind up in comas, and those two idiots are unharmed."

Thunder said dryly, "They were smart enough to run away."

Ashley said, "Well, I'm glad they're okay. Okay, so, is there a room we can have until we're ready to go? And food? My God, I could kill for real seafood."

"Yeah, I'll set it up," said Little Jack with a laugh.

Geneva suddenly arrived, looking very sad. But she smiled on seeing her friends. "Are you two going home?"

"For a visit. Then we're going to help you. Us Martian prisoners have to stay together," said Ashley with a laugh.

"Thank you. You have no idea how I value your bravery."

"Stop," said Ashley, blushing.

"I did all the hard work," said Thunder.

Geneva said, "I was told by the judges they did all the real heavy lifting."

They all cracked up at that. Then Geneva said to Little Jack, "You realize they are wandering around on that island with information only a handful of people in the world show know."

Thunder interjected before Little Jack could reply and aid, "Bloody codgers, who are they gonna tell, the frogs?"

Then they all laughed.

Something none of them had done so loudly for a long, long time.

Chapter Thirteen
Geneva and Lon

"This might be the only time I've been happy to be in Cleveland," said Lon to the desk clerk at a Sheraton Inn near the airport the next day He loosened his black tie, looking for a change a bit disheveled.

The clerk was a young brunette with a frowny mouth. She looked at him and said, "I'm from here. I like it here."

"Uh, sorry," said Lon, quickly paying with his VISA. Then he took his receipt and key, checked his watch, and turned.

Just as he did so, his wife walked through the large glass doors leading to the outside.

He froze, stunned with joy and love at the same time. Geneva was not considered, in general, a gorgeous woman. Yes, she was pretty. But to Lon, she was perfect, for he loved her and everything about her.

She wore olive pants with a turquoise skirt over them, a gray sweater, and a white sweatshirt that presently was unzipped. All in all, it was a typical airline outfit for Geneva, who liked to be comfortable on a plane. Her shoes were white heels with streaks of olive green as well. Her luggage was her purse.

As she entered, she wasn't looking for him. She was looking at her phone for the itinerary. She was on her way to Maine after making the stopover in Cleveland. They were spending the afternoon and evening together there. Lon was in the middle of a heated mission as a member of the Secret Service, but they had sprung him for a day.

Geneva would leave the next morning for Maine spend a few days resting and recovering with her family and some other friends, like Colin, who was coming out via separate flight. There was little she could do in terms of the search for Calico's team, and despite her dramatic increase in powers since her return from Hell in 2017, she was exhausted.

Those problems were for the future. This night was about husband and wife.

Looking up, she saw him staring at her, bemused by shock, joy, and love. She didn't realize it, but the look on her face was the same.

He had luggage, an overnight case. He left it and ran across the lobby, footsteps echoing on the tile. Dodging an elderly couple from Columbus and a young boy from Stuartville, he grabbed her, kissed her passionately, and held her in his arms for what felt like forever.

Geneva loved being held by him.

Finally, she said, "Need air."

He let her go. Both of them were crying. They were so overcome by their reunion that they couldn't speak.

When Geneva had gone to Hell, she had been single. She came back in love with Tripper. He did not feel anything for her. Shortly afterwards, she met Lon.

This separation from Lon wasn't heir first. They both had high stress jobs with travel. But it was the first forced separation, and it had been long, several months. She wasn't sure he would still love her.

That had been a foolish thought.

Finally, he spoke. "I have our room. Where are your clothes?"

"We'll buy some."

"Let's go upstairs first," he said.

"Certainly."

They were in a penthouse suite, a gift from Sylvester. The place was gorgeous with furniture, a huge bed, a spa, and a view of . . . well, the airport. The room was decorated in black, pink and white, giving it a weirdly candyish feel.

As soon as they were in the door, they held each other for what felt like a blissful eternity.

"My God, I've missed you."

She smiled. "I have missed you, too."

"I didn't think you were coming back."

She put a finger to his lips. "No more of that. It's over. It may happen again. I get around. You married a loose woman — dimensionally speaking."

He laughed. "Let's go to bed."

Laughing, she pulled him to the bed and said, "Sure. I could use a nap."

He hit her with a pillow.

Then they made love well into the night, never enjoying each other as much as in this moment.

They didn't sleep.

"You're pretty vibrant for a dead guy," said Geraldine Kane to the parallel Colin Ridgeway the next day in Maine.

"I get that a lot in this dimension," said Colin with a grin. He wore a straw hat, a yellow vest over an orange shirt, and brown pants. He looked a bit like a schizophrenic farmer.

They were gathered in the secondary dining room, a rustic design that hadn't changed since Geneva was a child. Geneva loved visiting her mom at the bed and breakfast her parents ran in the York area of Maine, but on this visit the team had gathered with her family for a long weekend at her grandparents' old home, a historical lighthouse. Geraldine also cared for that. Geneva's late grandparents, Gerald and Mary, had been her best friends as a child. Gerald taught her channeling when Geneva was sixteen and rescued her dog from drowning in the Atlantic, showing her first signs of her considerable elemental channeling ability. She had lived with them for a time after she discovered her channeling abilities so Gerald could train her.

Geneva's mom, Geraldine, had been a channeler injured in a battle with Reddy Otero in 1988. Since then, Geraldine and her husband, Joseph, had raised her family, Geneva and Geneva's flighty three-year younger sister, Medina. But Medina and Geneva's father got along well, and they were engaged in running their own financial investment businesses and some other operations. Medina was something of a marketing whiz.

Geraldine was now fifty-five, and she looked like an older version of Geneva, just with graying hair cut short and more wrinkles. Essentially, she was the guardian of the lighthouse now.

Medina was a pretty woman of thirty, very different from Geneva. She was a little chunky around the waist, but generally hid that with fashionable clothes. Her blonde hair was kept straight and long, parted in the middle and held back with hair-pins. She had wide, bright blue eyes, and always wore a lot of mascara and make-up. Her blush was light pink, and her preferred lipstick was bright red.

Joseph Kane was a well-built man of fifty-one who had graying brown hair, brown eyes, and a jutting jaw. He was the type of man who always looked relaxed, mostly because he always was. His career had been made in advertising, but now he was a financial consultant.

The kitchen itself was rustic with dark wooden cabinets, a light yellow refrigerator and dishwasher, and curtains with prints of roses. It was large, the central fixture a circular dinner table large enough to seat twelve. Presently, it was buried in enough food to feed Thanksgiving dinner for about forty.

Geneva had arrived earlier in the day, walked along the beach and talked to her mom, and taken a shower. She wore a white turtleneck, jeans, and royal blue booties with yellow stripes that were, of course, new. She took a bread roll to go with her huge meal and said, "It is . . . it is so good to be with my family and friends. I love you all so much, and I've missed you so much."

Colin raised a wine glass. "To the best of the best, the Kanes!"

They all toasted and cheered.

Geraldine put the last tray on the table, a plate of twice-baked potatoes, and had her seat. Then she said, "Let's pray."

They linked hands and Geneva said, "Thank you, Lord, for returning me safe to family and friends, for giving us Colin, for giving us a chance to stop those that would damage us all. Let us . . . let us resolve this conflict with them without more damage. Amen."

There was silence for a moment, then Geraldine saw the frown on her daughter's face. "You seem distressed, Geneva."

Geneva nodded. "I was . . . just thinking about Calico."

"Thinking?"

Geneva paused, then spoke to everyone. "I have a lot of concern about Calico . . . don't take me wrong, but I respect her . . . her drive, her intelligence. Her objective is sound. It's her method that's all wrong, and she can't see it. And so, on another level, because of that, she greatly scares me. She's very dangerous."

"I'm a lot more scared by the floating ball that eats souls," said Medina, making a face, having been brought up to date on events by Colin.

"A wise sibling," said Colin.

Geneva shook her head. "Of course. But ultimately, Quotient is a tool of Calico, that's all. He's just a big power source with catastrophic unintended consequences. Our real opponent, with Kelkirk dead, is Calico."

"Calico *is* a formidable opponent," said Colin grimly.

"Yes. She's fighting for what she believes is a good and noble cause, and the cause itself, well, it is a good cause. She is smart, skilled, and loyal to her team. They are her family as you are my family. She came from a family of channelers, one of whom was one of the greatest of his line. In many ways, we're mirror images of the other. Already in this battle we have lost Sheila Warren, Crystal Taylor, Meredith . . . poor Meredith . . . and Mary and Jen are in a coma. Marrina has been deposed and bodily converted back into Heidi Minor and the Mind of the Gods has abandoned us. And we've barely started the fight."

"Calico *isn't* like you, Geneva. She's immoral. She's killed many people by turning Quotient loose like a crazed bulldog. She lives by a code, yes, all people do. But the code benefits her aims and ignores all other concerns," said Colin grimly and angrily.

Geneva nodded. "Of course. And she murdered Meredith — in the heat of battle. But she isn't just *randomly* killing. That's important. They went to all the effort to set up a prison on Mars to avoid killing people. It's almost like she sees deaths to Quotient as a byproduct of a natural disaster . . . as if it is so well-ordained her plan must be law that those deaths don't count." She paused. "I'm sure she reconciles Meredith's death the same way. It was an instant reaction in battle."

"But those deaths do count," said Geraldine.

"I know that. *But she doesn't*. Anyhow . . . she will be very hard to stop."

"But we will," said Colin with a wink.

"I know that," said Geneva. She paused, ate, then sighed.

"What?" asked Medina.

Finally, Geneva said, "I just wish we knew where *Radar* was and what he was up to."

Colin chuckled. "He is a seer. Remember, he has to work objectives we know nothing about."

"I know. But it's annoying," she said, making a face. "I suspect he has answers . . . but where is he and who is he after?"

"He'll tell us in due course," said Colin confidently.

Geneva smiled at her mother, then said to Medina and Colin, "I'm really tired. I'm going to just lay on the couch and watch TV for a bit."

"Toodles, then. We'll be out in a bit. I have plenty of wine and delicious bread rolls to finish," said Colin with a smile, holding up the bottle to prove his point.

"Yeah, you rest up," said Medina.

Geneva exited to the living room. Geraldine said, "I'll sit with her a bit. Once you two are done, you can clean up."

Medina laughed. "Oh, mother, let's not be silly."

Geraldine laughed.

When they were gone, Colin smiled like a man with a secret and stared at Medina. Medina smiled like a woman with a secret and stared at Colin.

He then reached over and poked her nose as she sat still and said, "You're up to something."

"Yep."

"What did you want to talk about?"

She sipped her wine and smiled. "Things."

"Things?"

She folded her arms on the table and said, "The Colin of our world, bless him, trained my sister for Ops years ago." She paused. "I need a trainer. I want you."

Colin smiled. "I am most utterly sincerely flattered, but why not your beloved sister?"

Medina made a face as if she had stepped in cat vomit. "Oh, that didn't go so well last time. I mean, that was three years ago, and I don't think I was really quite ready." She looked very earnest now. "But I've changed. I run a lot of things for dad, and more importantly, the world has changed. My sister got sucked to Hell. She got zapped to Mars. I need to be able to take care of things if . . . God forbid . . . one time she doesn't come back."

Now Colin looked serious as well. "That is a noble gesture."

"My family is important to me. And, well, aside from the whole sister thing, Geneva has more than enough on her plate." She laughed and added, "You're basically freeloading in our dimension getting free bread rolls. You can earn your keep!"

He laughed heartily, jumped up, clapped his hands, then moved over and extended his hand. She shook it and he said, "We are now officially a team."

"A covert team. No one else knows. Got it?"

"Got it. Of all things a Ridgeway can manage, keeping a secret ranks right up there with hearty eating and robust, manic energy!"

She smiled. "I take it you're always this way?"

"Indeed. Most certainly!"

Medina leaned back and folded her arms over her chest. "Boy, then this is gonna be interesting. I think you'll do a much better job than my sister."

Chapter Fourteen
Laid To Rest

Geneva awakened at three in the morning and threw her head back with a scream. It wasn't a terribly loud scream, just a jarring one.

She sat up in bed. She was sleeping in a spare room that now housed all of her grandfather's old drawing boards, blue drawing chair, original art, and a spare bed. Gerald had drawn comics for decades, including his main claim to fame, *Black Flashlight*.

Using her right hand, she pushed the hair out of her eyes and slowly got out of bed. The lighthouse air conditioning was turned off, but it was only sixty-six outside, so she was comfortable. The air was a little humid. She had a clip fan on the headboard, and she turned it on and just sat for a moment, orienting herself. Wearing a turquoise, full length nightgown, she slowly rose.

She'd been having a nightmare, seeing Meredith cut in half by giant scissors. She didn't need a therapist to figure out where that came from.

Slowly, she rose and slipped on some black yoga pants under her nightgown and noticed it was 3:12 in the morning. She went downstairs. The house was quiet and mostly dark, though her mother had nightlights in each room. One of the two long-haired black cats, came to check out what she was doing, but rapidly lost interest and scurried away.

Geneva took an entire bottle of grape juice from the refrigerator and brought it back upstairs, but she moved past the drawing room and went to the main room used for maintenance of the lighthouse. There was a catwalk ringing it and there were chairs. She sat on one and stared out into the Atlantic. The light for the lighthouse was active, mostly just for show. It was historical and no longer had any function, but part of maintaining the non-profit status was running the light.

She sat for a time, drinking the grape juice from the bottle, her feet up on the metal rail. She noticed it had recently been repainted gray. She smiled. Her mother took good care of the facility.

The ocean was calm. The light drowned out many of the stars, but she could see some. She loved staring out at the ocean.

Meredith . . .

"Geneva?"

Geneva was startled. She turned to see her mother, wearing a white robe and a second apricot bathrobe over it, looking worried.

"Hi, mom. Sorry, did I wake you?"

"I heard what I thought was a scream and heard you get up. I gave it a few minutes . . . are you okay?"

Geneva slid a chair close to her, and her mother sat down as she said, "I haven't sat up and here and watched the ocean in a long time. I would do this sometimes when gramps was drawing when I was a kid."

"I know. Usually when you were sad."

Geneva nodded. Then she felt herself starting to cry, but she took a deep breath and didn't. She said, "Meredith . . . we told her to wait. She ignored us. She stopped them. She killed Nile and stopped the spell. But she . . . we couldn't do anything. We were too far away, it happened to fast. She was killed right in front of us." She didn't look at her mother. She kept staring at the ocean and shook her head. "It . . . hasn't really hit me yet. I had a nightmare about it."

"I'm sorry, honey. I wish I could help."

Geneva sipped the grape juice. "Mother, your love always helps. But sometimes, well, you just have to go through the pain."

"I understand."

Geneva knew her mother did. She loved her very, very much.

After a few minutes, Geraldine asked, "Is Sam going to take care of Meredith's . . . I mean, it must be a little odd."

"Yes. I offered to go, but he said it was silly to have a second funeral just to, you know, put her real body in place. He said Jameson and Searly would go with him."

"No one has found Chase?" she asked. Chase Meridian, a veteran Ops agent, had been kidnapped in February and hadn't been seen or heard from since.

"No. I mean . . . I think they hoped maybe Calico kidnapped her and she was with me. But we never saw her." She paused. "I'm very worried about her. I'm worried about everything, mother. Calico is very dangerous. This . . . this may be too much for me."

"Easy, honey. You're just grieving." She patted her daughter on the knee. "And you're full of sugar."

Geneva laughed and held up her empty juice bottle. "I know. I've fallen off the wagon!"

"It's nice to see you smile. It's just . . . hell, it's just nice to see you."

They hugged. Then Geneva said, "Calico is just . . . when grandfather was training me at first, he'd talk some about the Nazis. I mean, he would when he was drawing and I was little and playing with dolls, too. It always struck me . . . how it struck him . . . how the Nazis weren't . . . they just believed they were right. They justified what they did under the belief that what they had was the only solution." She paused. "Calico is the same way. She believes she has the only solution. So she believes whatever pain it causes justifies it." She paused again. "She could have been a real *good* person, mother. But somewhere deep inside, she's . . . skewed."

"Her father probably didn't help," offered Geraldine.

"True." Pause. "I've thought about . . . trying to play along, trying to reason with her, get her to see maybe we can do all this without Quotient! Or do something." Pause. "She killed Meredith. I can . . . I can understand that. It was the heat of battle. And Meredith was not someone they expected to see and not at that time, certainly. But stealing people's *souls* . . . is ghoulish. It's worse than the gas chambers. At least the Nazis just killed the body."

Geraldine said, "It sickens me, and you cannot reason with these people, honey. To go this far, they are beyond the line."

Geneva nodded slowly. "I know. I just . . . we've lost Jen, Mary, Meredith, and Crystal so far. This is . . . this is going to be a costly endeavor."

"I know. So was world War II. But it saved the world. And you and your friends have to do so as well."

Geneva nodded. "I wish Meredith were here . . . Colin told me about something she told him happened to her when Zenith held her captive. It's . . . it's really upset me, I think, more than I thought."

"Do you want to talk about it?"

Geneva paused. Colin had told her how Meredith, who had been in prison and told Colin as her defense attorney in the parallel world, when captured by Zenith in Illinois Meredith had been forced to drink the liquified corpse of a guard. She did not want to burden her mother with this information. "Just sit with me a bit, mom. That's all I really need now."

"Sure."

And then Geneva started to cry.

She cried for several minutes. Her mother held her the way only a mother can, comforting and nurturing.

Finally, Geneva said with a look of cold determination, "We will stop her, mother. We have to."

"I know."

"But it's going to cost us. Meredith isn't going to be the last one to die."

"It kind of takes someone like Meredith to die twice," said Sam a few hours later and thousand miles west, shaking his head as he stared down at the unearthed and replanted grave of Meredith Patience.

Meredith, of course, had originally been buried without a corpse. She was next to her mother, father, and sister — her sister also buried without a corpse. Zenith had destroyed it.

They were in a small cemetery in Lake Forest, Illinois, an upscale northern suburb that had been the home of such Chicago luminaries as Mike Ditka and Michael Jordan. The city was along Lake Michigan in Lake County, just north of the Cook County border, and had a small population of 20,000. This was also where Meredith was born and raised.

The three graves were crucifix shaped and very expensive. They had no sayings, just names and dates. Sam had kept Meredith's grave in the pattern of the rest of the family.

There were three people at the site: Sam; his former boss and former Director of Special Operations until his firing in 214 General Emerald Jon Jameson; and Ops paranormal agent Searly McTaggert. Sam wore a black suit, as did Jameson. Searly wore a black, full length dress.

Jameson snorted. "Meredith had quite the life."

Sam put flowers on her grave. "I don't know why I bother. She was never sentimental. She'd been through too much grief."

"I'm sure she'd appreciate them," said Jon.

"I'm sure she'd roll her eyes at them," said Sam with a smile.

Searly moved forward and put a white rose on the grave. "I'm really sorry that . . . well, you know."

She stepped back and turned to Sam. "We've been friends a long time, Sam. You know I was upset about Meredith's behavior. But I guess . . . in the end . . . you proved me wrong. She was worth saving. She saved everyone on the island."

Sam nodded and said, "Everyone is worth saving, Searly, if they want to be saved. And she did. She just didn't know how to do it without eliminating all the . . . threats."

Jameson said, "It's water over the bridge now. I just find it strange that she lived and died again . . . it's not a typical thing."

"Yeah, it's odd, but then what isn't in our lives?"

"In anyone's life," added Searly.

Then Searly stood between the two of them and looked at Jon. "General . . . Jon . . . I was just a teenager when you found me in Cairo. I was scared and confused and . . . Kathie had been turned into Quafara and I had powers and Carlie had been killed and I had a stroke and . . . it was just crazy. But you were always there for me." She looked at Sam. "And when Clarke," and she smiled at his memory, "when he . . . when we married, and then when it all happened, you and Bam were so good to me, Sam. And so was Meredith, in her way." She looked resolute. "These people, the Kelkirks, her friends . . . they are monsters. They always were. We have to stop them."

"I know," said Sam, and he hugged her. They didn't hug romantically, more like brother and sister.

Then she hugged Jameson and said, "I never knew life could be so hard."

"It isn't always . . . it won't be always." He paused, then said, "Searly, I probably never told you this, but I lost my first love to a vampire. That's what got me into this business. I know what it's like to lose in the paranormal game."

"I'm sorry for you, Jon," she said sincerely.

"Thanks, but I just wanted you to know that . . . there are better days. There are always better days. It will not always be like this."

"I hope not," she said, clearly less than convinced.

Then she hugged him.

When they broke the hug, Searly said, "Sam, they must have taken Chase, too. She was dangerous to them even without her channeling. But where would they have her?"

"I don't know," said Sam sadly. He nodded at the grave. "Geneva didn't see her in Germany or Mars and finding Kelkirk's home is basically impossible." He paused, not wanting to get into explaining how the random tachyon field laced with probability cloud particles made it appear to be everywhere and nowhere at once. "Chase always supported Meredith. She understood Meredith. I wish Meredith were here for many reasons, but that's one of them. She might have an idea where Chase is or what she's going through or how to find her."

Jameson said, "Or not. I'm just sad she's gone . . . again."

"Yeah," said Sam. "We should head back. I mean . . . I can always visit."

Of course, in another month or so, he wouldn't be able to say that, but he didn't know that yet.

"Sam, can we go get something to eat? I just don't want to be alone now," said Searly.

"I don't think I do either."

Jameson said, "You can't do it without me. I'm buying." He moved between them and put his arms over their shoulders. "We'll just be in the moment for a while. I'll call Little Jack later and let him know I'm expensing the bill."

"Jack? Are you okay?" asked Joy from the doorway leading into his office at Ops' headquarters in Las Vegas.

He was staring out the window at the mountains east of Vegas, not a normal position. He wasn't a pensive man. But he looked somber, left arm up on the window, leaning his forehead on it, his nose hitting the glass. His dress was his typical pin-striped gray and black dress shirt with jeans, but the shirt was completely untucked.

"Yeah, I guess." He tried to push her off and said, "I just signed the check for the next six months of this random anti-matter tachyonic field that keeps Quotient from popping onto the complex. It cost nearly a billion bucks. Although we think he's probably on Mars now. A satellite got a signature tachyonic wave from Mars' surface."

"I see," she said. "That's not usually what you think about while staring at the window."

He said nothing.

Joy moved into the room slowly. She wore a black and pink wraparound one-piece bathing suit. "I was going to go for a swim and try to work out some stuff, but I think you need to talk."

"Nah. Go have fun."

She moved behind him and put her hands around his torso. Gently, she said, "I know you're a private man. I know you've seen things you can't talk about. But I think you should try. If nothing else, it will help me understand you better."

He smiled and turned to her. "You're way too good for me."

Seriously, she said, "No, not at all. I just see the real Jack inside this . . . persona."

Studying her, he said, "It's . . . it's Meredith. I just . . . her being found alive, then being dead . . . it's stirred up some memories of . . . the *old* me."

Concerned but not panicked, she said, "I'm sure that is the case. We all have feelings about her."

"Because you were her friends. I was her enemy. I . . . don't like to think about who I was before the portal, Joy."

"That's because that man *wasn't* you. What happened to you rewired your brain, Jack, and more importantly your soul. Mary told us this." She hugged him. "Don't feel like that man, because that man died in Arizona."

"I remember . . . the things I did. They were . . . I was not a man without morals or ethics. But the moral or ethic was always to close the deal."

She looked up at him, a tiny bird. "Do you want to tell me what you did? It won't change my opinion of you, because it wasn't you, and it might help to talk."

"I'm sure it's in the files anyhow . . . I . . . it's just hard to admit some of the things the McGrath guy, the old me, did. Because . . . you're right, I rebuilt my . . . soul . . . along with my brain . . . it's hard to explain. But I guess the best comparison is the Bible. You know about Paul and Saul?"

"No, not really," said Joy. She wasn't Christian, though she believed in God, and hadn't gone to Sunday school much at all.

"Saul persecuted Christians in Roman times. He was the ultimate anti-Christian bad-ass. Then he got hit by lightning and had a complete personality change, as apparently God talked to him and asked him why he persecuted his people? Saul converted one-hundred percent and became Paul, one of the great Christians."

"Like you."

Little Jack nodded. "Like me. But I still *remember* what I did. I tried to kill Meredith. I tried hard. I took a couple hostages and set a trap. They were terrified . . . all of them. Meredith beat me, refused to play by my rules." He smiled. "She always had her own way of looking at things." Then he looked terribly sad. "But . . . I did those things. I used people as objects, as means to an end."

"I'm so sorry," she said softly.

He turned and kicked the side of the wall under the window and shouted, "Don't feel sorry for me, god damn it! *Be angry with me*! I'm fucking disgusting and hate myself! How could I have done those things?"

And then he fell to his knees and grabbed her legs.

Sobbing, he wailed, "How could I have done those things?"

She had no answer.

So she merely held him.

Chapter Fifteen
Lost at Sea
June 1, 2020

"Oh, yeah, baby, that feels so nice," said Sasha, groaning as Hickory lay between her legs, giving her oral satisfaction.

With long, chestnut hair, blue eyes, and a body that wouldn't quit, Hickory looked up and smiled. "This is the best."

Lanky Sasha brushed her long, black hair out of her eyes and said, "You know that, baby. Now get back to licking. I'm really into it now that we absorbed her."

With that, Sasha pointed to the large, circular table to their left. On top of it lay Kia Zhong, a teenager they had kidnapped on leaving Honolulu, a toy for their TM games. Kia had finally died a few minutes earlier, her body covered in bruises, wounds, and punctures from broken bones. Her dead eyes stared endlessly at the birds beginning to circle above.

They lay on the deck of the yacht owned by their boss, German TM, Consortium member, and crime-lord Julian Hahn, loving the sun and salty air . . . and each other. Julian had gone below deck to mix more drinks.

The Arrow was a sixty-foot yacht, but it was manned completely by Julian and his two female acolytes, Hickory and Sasha. Julian was a firm believer in automation, and their TM powers enabled them to handle emergencies like microbursts or rough seas.

Both women were twenty-four and had been found by Julian during one of his Consortium meetings in Prague. They looked very similar. Hickory had long, brown hair parted in the middle and straight with blue eyes and a narrow face and frame. Sasha was much the same, but she had red highlights in her hair, wider eyes, and more fullness in the lips, tits, and hips, as Julian would say.

They had sailed together many times the past five years and were prepared for anything the ocean could throw at them.

What they *weren't* prepared for was Radar.

Sasha lay back on her pink reclining chair. Both women wore sunglasses, hiding their blue eyes, but Sasha had removed her bikini while Hickory still wore her pink two-piece. Their bodies were slick with suntan lotion and glistened in the brilliant mid-day sun.

Radar came aboard on the far side, behind the main cabin. Once aboard, he watched the two women from around the corner. Then he stepped forward.

"Hi, ladies. You know the way to San Jose?"

Sasha gasped in shock. Before her stood, well . . . a robot? Glistening gold in color, it was about six feet tall, with a round head and a torso shaped like a pot belly stove. Extendable tentacles that looked like metal vacuum cleaner hoses connected the torso to metal hands and feet that looked like part of a child's toy more than a sophisticated machine. The robot was compact and buxom, like an offensive tackle, in the head and torso, but the arms and legs were thin and skinny. That it didn't tip over was amazing. Oh, and it had no neck.

Despite her shock, Hickory acted, stepping back and rolling to her right while using TK to hurl a fire extinguisher at the intruder. It struck Radar, had no effect, and with a loud KLANG bounced harmlessly into the Pacific to entertain some fish.

Radar moved quickly. He channeled wind to lift the women up and slam their heads together in a painful collision. In the middle of their sex and vacationing, the two TMs were taken completely by surprise.

Once they lay on the deck, he checked their vitals. They were out. Removing a needle from one of the compartments on his metal body, he drugged them to make sure they remained unconscious. Then he found some rope, plentiful on the deck of the ship, and tied them with their hands behind their backs to the table, which was a solid metal object bolted into the deck by the women, who had used it as their torture platform earlier. It had to be sturdy to withstand the escape attempts of their victim.

The victim was obviously dead. Radar shook his head, shut her eyes, and said, "I promise, lady, you won't be forgotten."

Then Radar sat on the reclining chair and put his hands behind his head. Using his internal communications, he hacked into the yacht's sound system and the classic country and western of the Oak Ridge Boys began flowing through the speakers.

Julian arrived moments later, carrying a tray of vodka and cocaine. He was the vodka man, the girls were into the coke. Snarling, he pushed open the door from the cabin and marched out as if a stormtrooper as he snapped in a distinct, staccato German accent, "What are you two sluts doing? That music is . . . awful."

Seeing Radar, Julian simply dropped the tray and stared, wide-eyed. Julian was fifty-six with gray hair, a chubby face, and an arrogant air. Tall at six-two, he was a little overweight but in reasonable shape for his age. His eyes were a dark brown and he had big ears, his only negative feature. Wearing a white and blue Hawaiian shirt and no pants, his ruddy color faded instantly on seeing Radar.

Radar turned and said, "I'll take the vodka, but you can keep the coke. That stuff ain't good for ya."

Although one of Europe's most formidable TMs, Julian had been taken *completely* by surprise. Radar channeled, and a wave came over the edge of the ship and shoved Julian into the far side, knocking him out and washing him to Radar.

Radar chuckled, tied Julian up between Hickory to his left and Sasha to his right, and waited. He checked the news. He also sent a message about NASA to General Lester Shank, head of the WSA, who was currently in Dallas.

Seventeen minutes later, Julian woke up.

"Mein gott," he said, seeing Radar standing looking down on them.

"Nah, I'm just a guy named John from Illinois," said Radar. "But feel honored. I mean, it isn't for just anyone I'd sit around in the ocean for five or six days and float like a leftover beer can. Lucky thing I don't rust or sunburn."

"What . . . are you?" asked Julian in a whisper.

"I'm what your ol' buddy Hitler wanted back in the day. A robot warrior."

"Mein gott," said Julian again. Then he said with slight offense, "I am no Nazi."

Radar chuckled, which sounded very sinister in his electronic voice. "Aw, Julian, your family was thicker than fleas on a dog with the Nazis. And your family has *always* been up to something." Then Radar leaned forward and smiled. "Which is good, because I'm going to need some help."

Julian frowned. "Help? What are you? A TM as well?"

"I told you, I'm a robot. But I have a real mind in this body. My body was destroyed, and I gotta get back at those that did it. You know everyone in Europe on the shady side. You help me find 'em, and I won't turn you into pudding. Deal?"

Glaring, Julian said, "I wish to hear more, but I am willing to listen."

"Good. Then we can get to business without me giving ya a spanking first."

Chapter Sixteen
The Dead Girl is Not So Much Dead

On June 4, 2020, Ted Bundt entered his large penthouse office in the skyscraper that served as the headquarters of World Marine Casualty Insurance — the largest division of the world's largest insurer, Meridian Insurance — in Berlin. Ted was a pretty typical looking, middle-aged man of 57, with short-cut gray hair, sagging jowls, and lots of moles. He was wearing a very expensive, stylish gray suit. As he walked down a marble-tiled corridor through an expensive entryway filled with glass cases that held rare art and other artifacts, he was studying the mail his receptionist had left in a drop box for him before she went to the restroom. Engrossed in the mail, he did not notice the fact that someone was sitting in his very expensive. Marble desk that was lined with gold trim.

"Mein Gott!"

"Nah, just me, Radar," said Radar, who was sitting at his desk with his hands crossed behind his head and his feet on the desk.

Stunned, Ted dropped the mail on the floor as the door automatically shut behind him. He looked around, and suddenly he saw flanking the door behind him Hickory and Sasha. They were wearing expensive executive business outfits: Hickory wore a black skirt with a polka dot blouse and Sasha wore a green skirt and jacket over white hose.

Each woman wore a black choker connected with a red jewel. They were elegant and went with the outfits, but they were really slave collars Radar had put on them, collars well disguised. With the chokers in place, the woman couldn't use their paranormal powers — but, of course, Ted didn't know this.

The women he recognized, so he was less alarmed, but he was still astonished by Radar's presence. "What *are* you?"

Radar chuckled and turned off the Johnny Cash music he had been streaming through robotic body. "I'm just a guy lookin' for insurance, Ted, and Julian gave me your info."

Ted now felt emboldened, for he was not a normal executive despite his executive appearance. He had been a TM a long time, a clandestine one who flew under the radar. Effectively protected by the Consortium, due to his value as a worldwide insurance provider, he had gained considerable power without giving up much. He was protected.

Turning to the women, he asked, "Where is our friend Julian?"

Hickory smiled. "He couldn't make it. Business in France."

Ted made a face. "Awful place."

"There we agree, bud," said Radar, looking relaxed as if he were planning to have a beer.

Cautiously, Ted moved a few feet into the office, leaving plenty of space between him and the robot, but also showing that he wasn't afraid.

The two women behind him cautiously flanked the door, preventing his escape. But that wasn't necessary, as Ted was far too curious about Radar to be frightened anyhow.

Ted said, "Well, you could've just called my receptionist and gotten an appointment. We have great rates this time of year, although I'm not entirely sure of our price structure for robots. Rust, you know."

Radar chuckled. "You and I both know I'm not here for rust insurance buddy. I'm here because of Sternvogel."

Ted showed no reaction to the name, other than he merely shrugged and said, "Robot, I don't know what you mean."

Radar smiled, "You can call me Radar, bud. You sure you don't know what I mean? We're going to have a talk about Sternvogel in the coming days.

Ted said, "Why would that happen?"

Radar chuckled and said, "Because you carry the commercial insurance on Sternvogel's tour. And because of that you have access to her that nobody else has. And since you're a torture magician and a major figure in the Consortium, well, that makes me a little suspicious about what you're up to."

"I am what I am robot, but what are you?"

"That's for me to know." He rose and said, "Me and the girls thought we'd just stop in while Julian took care of some other business. See, this is just a friendly little chat, a friendly little visit to establish that we're gonna have a working relationship over the next few weeks. Meaning, I'll be running this place, and if you raise one word of alarm to the Consortium, well, you'll find that robots can make life very unpleasant. That work for you?"

Ted studied him. He was an arrogant, vain man, but he was also highly placed in the Consortium and had led a pretty cushy life the past decade. He decided to play this out a bit. "Well, I guess it has to, doesn't it?"

Radar chuckled as he rose and started moving towards the door. "Well, it's nice to see you're cooperative. We'll see if that holds up when I start giving you tasks."

Ted looked at the two women. Both women looked at him and shook their heads with light eyes, making it quite clear they were afraid and that this was not a joke. Ted took that non-verbal communication very seriously. He was a smart, disciplined man, which had made him a success. He wasn't about to take a foolish risk in a wild act of machismo.

"I think it will. But what is your interest in the affairs of the Consortium?"

"None. You guys can run the planet into the ground like a bad bus stop for all I care. I just want the kid."

Ted nodded. "That seems fair."

Radar walked passed him, gestured to the women to follow, then paused at the door. "Don't get any fancy ideas. I've planted bio-weapons and trackers. I know what you do every minute and can kill you from miles away, and if I'm here, well, I come fully equipped with weapons," and he held up a metal finger, "and a built-in microwave. I can kill ya while I cook dinner."

"I can understand your need. I have no wish to, as Americans would say, make waves. I will cooperate."

As he exited, the girls flanking him, Radar said, "Good. I'll be in touch."

"Danke."

"Right back at ya, Ted."

Once in the corridor, Hickory said, "He *will* cooperate. We've worked with him. Julian has known him since they were at university."

"He better. Now, you two head back to the hotel and work on those financial papers I gave you. I gotta make one other stop."

"As you desire. It's not like we have a choice," said Sasha bitterly, and with her German accent she sounded like a pouting child.

Radar met her glare. "Neither did any of those junior high kids you tortured to death."

"I will punish you for this indignity," snapped Sasha.

Radar smiled. "Don't make threats you can't keep, kid." Then he sent an electric surge through the collar.

"Stop!" cried Sasha, her neck on fire, the fire burning down her spine and up into her head. "I apologize!"

"Good. Now move your ass."

With that, he entered the stairwell while they proceeded to the elevator bay. Radar reached the roof. The door to the roof was locked, but he simply smashed the lock and stepped onto the tar.

Lost in thought, Radar walked across the roof and was shocked to hear a female voice.

"Hey, Big Gold, what's your hurry?"

He turned to see a young woman of perhaps twenty leaning against the eight-foot-tall steel wall that blocked off the air conditioning unit. She had one leg up and the foot planted on the wall, the other down, and her arms were folded and pushing forward her cleavage. Her dress was unusual — white boots that extended about hallway up her shin, white gloves that extended to the elbows, and a white onesie that had three circles on each side cut out. The onesie attached around her neck and fit her perfectly.

Cautiously, Radar stopped near the edge of a railing around the solar panels, about ten feet away. He was wary. Nothing in his systems or his channeling ability to detect auras picked up *anything* from this woman. It was as if she didn't exist.

To her he said, "I rust if I stay out in the rain. Who're you?"

She cocked her head and turned away, as if flirting with him in a club. "Julie Julian."

"Never heard of you."

She smiled and it was sexy and dark. "A pity. I guess a girl who gets kidnapped gets forgotten after three years." She paused, Radar had no reaction, so she continued and coyly said, "You're John Patience. I've wanted to meet you." She arched an eyebrow, and her smile became coy.

"I go by Radar now, and I'm not lookin' to hook up, kid," he said, but he was running a link to Ops' database based on her name. What came back surprised him. As he watched her, data flowed through his eyepiece at the bottom of the 'screen,' telling him he was dealing with someone or something decidedly paranormal.

In 2017, Julie Julian had been a seventeen-year-old, middle-class white girl who was a senior at Poway High, outside San Diego, when her life changed. A Christian and a big fan of Supergirl, Julie was in superb shape and was a knock-out, a ritual work-out maven.

Today, she looked just as she had three years ago. At five feet and eight inches tall, she had legs and hips of pure muscle, and a butt that looked like a picture from a comic book. Despite her strength, she wasn't overtly muscular.

According to Ops files, Julie was always wound up and hyper. Sitting was boring. Presently, she was wearing a retro '80s hairdo. Her brown hair was teased and tightly curled, cut short but flaring wide, and swept to the right on her head. She also had dyed it to lighten the color, resulting in a few blonde streaks. Her lips were framed in light red lipstick, and her light blue eyes were highlighted by an eyelash treatment.

Julie had been kidnapped by the TM Trixie Taylor and taken to the Consortium, specifically Kelkirk and Calico, the father and daughter TM team running the Consortium. They had used her in a channeling experiment as a sacrifice, due to her unique affinity for the probability cloud, which was a tachyonic event that distorted probabilities in a localized field.

Julie died.

And then she woke up. The only reference Kelkirk received was that she had made contact with an entity called the Four Cornered Wheel, but Radar did not know this. Ops files ended with Julie being kidnapped and taken to Germany.

No one Ops associated with had seen or heard of her since that day in 2017.

"Oh? I hear you're lookin' for a girl," she said in a dark and sexy way, as if she were trying to secretly hook him up with her college roommate for a three-way.

"Maybe," said Radar.

Smiling with perfect teeth, coyly dropping her head, she said, "I see." Pointing at herself, she said, "But there's *something* I know," and she pointed at him, "that *you* don't."

"Really?"

Still smiling, she nodded as if she had a big secret and flashed her eyes at him.

"Kid, I'm rusting, and pigeons are shitting on me. What have you got?"

"I know ultimately you want to find Sternvogel."

"So?"

Looking around as if to make sure they weren't overheard, she put a finger to her mouth and then said, "I know where she is."

"So do I," lied Radar.

Smiling, Julie shook her head. "No, you don't, Radar. Oh, no. You think you do. But you also know that you see nothing in the future *after* her . . . manifestation."

Alarmed she knew so much about him, he said, "What makes ya think that, kid?"

Now she stood erect and sauntered sexily towards him, stopping two feet away. For Radar, all sound and movement had disappeared other than Julie. Her aura scan was completely unique compared to anything he'd seen before. There was a human aura. But dwarfing that was a tachyonic matrix inside an anti-matter field that indicated portaling, but the reading was light years beyond what should register for that.

"Because there is no future after her."

Radar said nothing.

Julie added, "But what counts, Big Gold, is I know how to *change* that."

As she looked at him, he said, "You're no woman."

"But I'm a lady," she said with a smile.

"No. What are you?"

"A conduit," she said. "And I am a woman. Julie is still here, a willing partner. We just borrow her form to communicate."

Radar doubted that, but he said nothing.

And after a moment's silence, she added, "And we are the only ones that can guide you through the calamity to come . . . the only ones that can guide *humanity* through the calamity to come."

www.ingramcontent.com/pod-product-compliance
Lightning Source LLC
Chambersburg PA
CBHW061538120726
48001CB00004B/1614